D0046481

Lost in Paris

Also by Cindy Callaghan
Just Add Magic
Lost in London
Lucky Me

Coming in summer 2015
Lost in Rome

Lost in Paris

CINDY CALLAGHAN

Aladdin
New York London Toronto Sydney New Delhi

ALADDIN
An imprint of Simon & Schuster Children's Publishing Division
1230 Avenue of the Americas, New York, NY 10020
This Aladdin hardcover edition March 2015
Text copyright © 2015 by Cindy Callaghan
Jacket illustration copyright © 2015 by Annabelle Metayer
Also available in an Aladdin M!X paperback edition.
For information about special discounts for bulk purchases,
please contact Simon & Schuster Special Sales at 1-866-506-1949
or business@simonandschuster.com.
The Simon & Schuster Speakers Bureau can bring authors to your live
event. For more information or to book an event contact
the Simon & Schuster Speakers Bureau at 1-866-248-3049
or visit our website at www.simonspeakers.com.
Jacket designed by Jessica Handelman
Interior designed by Hilary Zarycky
The text of this book was set in ITC Berkeley Oldstyle.
Manufactured in the United States of America 0215 FFG
2 4 6 8 10 9 7 5 3 1
Library of Congress Control Number 2014957772
ISBN 978-1-4814-4178-0 (hc)
ISBN 978-1-4814-2601-5 (pbk)
ISBN 978-1-4814-2602-2 (eBook)

Pour ma mère et mon père. Merci pour tout. Je vous aime.

Acknowledgments

Ooh la la, so many fab people to thank:

A writer girl can't do much without *formidable* critique partners and writing pals: Gale, Carolee, Josette, Jane, Chris, and Shannon, and the Northern Delaware Sisters in Crime group: John, KB, Jane, June, Chris, Janis, Susan, and Kathleen.

Special thanks to Chris Lally, the mastermind of plot, who always meets me when I'm in a panic. Many of the ideas incorporated herein came from her beautiful head.

Thanks to my friends, who are super supportive of this life and listen to me talk about fictitious people, places, and situations.

A thousand *merci*s to my literary dream team, who just "get" me: Mandy Hubbard, literary agent, and Alyson Heller, editor. Without them, none of this works.

As always, to my family: Ellie, Evan, Happy, Kevin, my parents, nieces and nephews, sister, sisters-in-law, brothers-in-law, and mother-in-law, thank you for your continued encouragement! Extra-special thanks to my daughter and Parisian travel-mate, Ellie, for sharing the City of Light with me. "We'll always have Paris."

To teachers, librarians, and most of all, my readers: I love getting your e-mails, letters, pictures, selfies, posts, and tweets. . . . Keep 'em coming! I hope you love *Lost in Paris* as much as *Lucky Me, Lost in London*, and *Just Add Magic*.

To all of you above, and those I've somehow forgotten (*pardon!*): *Je vous souhaite santé et bonheur!*

1

I traced my finger over the gold emblem of my new passport. It was blank, but it would have its first stamp very soon. A stamp that said FRANCE!

My brothers were playing in a lacrosse tournament overseas, which meant that I got to go to . . . *wait for it* . . . Paris!

While the boys were off playing lacrosse, Mom and I planned to tour the entire city—the City of Light. That was what they called Paris. What I wanted to do most of all was to take a boat ride down the Seine—that was the river that flowed through the center of the city. My dad had to stay behind for work, so he would miss all the fun. *Quel dommage!* That was "bummer" in French, I thought, or maybe it was "it's too bad," or "scrambled eggs."

Giddy with excitement, I placed the passport back onto the middle of the kitchen table, so everyone could see it. It had my name, Gwen Russell; my picture; and my birth date, indicating that I was thirteen. "It's beautiful, isn't it?" I asked Mom for the umpteenth time.

"Yes, it is. It'll look even better with a stamp in it." She looked at her cell phone. "The boys just texted. They'll be home soon with pizza."

By "boys" she meant my three older brothers. There were four kids in our family. I was the youngest and the only girl, the only one who stepped on the mat when she got out of the shower, the only one who took her shoes off at the door, and the only one who'd never traveled overseas. But not for long.

I pulled up the latest Shock Value video on my tablet and turned the sound waaaay up. I grabbed a broom, played air guitar, and sang along. I didn't sing when the boys were around because they told me I was terrible, but when they weren't around, I belted it out. I knew every word to this song.

Shock Value was only THE most amazing band, I

dreamed that one day I'd get tickets to one of their concerts. I wanted to see Winston up close. He was my total fave band member. Maybe because he was the youngest, but also because he was the cutest with a capital C. But I doubted I would ever get to see them in person, since tickets to their shows were like a bagillion dollars. A girl could still dream, and I did. I wasn't the only one nuts about Shock Value. My brothers and parents loved them too.

When the video was over, I played it again with the volume lower and jumped over the couch with a notebook in which I wrote song lyrics. I called it my Lyrics Notebook. Creative, huh? I jotted:

I'm going to Paris.
Café au lait.
I can't wait for France.
To stroll along the boulevards

I admired my work. Okay, so maybe these weren't the best lyrics, but I was getting better. Maybe one day I'd write a song for Shock Value.

As I studied my notebook, the door to the garage slammed open, and Josh (seventeen), Topher (sixteen), and Charlie (fifteen) walked in, each carrying a pizza box. The kitchen instantly filled with the smell of boy

3

sweat and garlic. They stacked their slices three high, grabbed extra-large Gatorades, and headed toward the stairs, where I knew they were about to play hallway lacrosse in between showers and burping.

"Come on, Gwen," Topher said on his way up. "We need a goalie."

The goalie was the one who kept the ball from rolling down the stairs.

"I'll be there in a little bit." I pointed to my mom. "Girl talk, you know."

"No. I don't know." He flew up the stairs two at a time.

I sighed.

I said to Mom, "Tell me again about the flight."

CRASH! It sounded like the ball had knocked something over.

"We're leaving tomorrow evening, and we'll fly all night on the red-eye," Mom said.

"AWW!" cried Josh. I was pretty sure he'd caught an elbow to the gut.

I ran up to see the boy drama. No one was dead.

I hung out, and as the hallway lacrosse game whirled around me, I put my earbuds in, played a Shock Value song, and imagined myself in front of each fab sight in Paris. Mom and I really needed some quality girl time. ASAP!

2

I'd never been on a plane ride that long before. It felt like I had just slept in a shoe box, but one glimpse of Paris and I didn't care.

As our taxi zoomed, with a capital Z, through the streets, the highway and buildings near the airport gave way to the Paris I had always imagined. The city was already alive with people in the middle of their morning routines. I could see the beautiful cobblestone streets lined with beautiful buildings that just screamed Paris—and definitely didn't look like Pennsylvania! All the storefronts had chic-looking everything: window displays, awnings, and shoppers—many with their dogs in tow.

Finally, we arrived at our hotel. The Hôtel de Paris lobby was small, cozy, and warm—maybe too warm—like, stuffy, and I wanted to open a window. In a modern city of glitz and fashion, the Hôtel de Paris felt like a time capsule from another century. The lights of the antique chandelier were dim, and a candle on the check-in desk reminded me of wildflowers. The drapes were heavy and dark, the furnishings were something out of a museum.

After a long late-afternoon nap (in four-poster beds) to recover from staying up all night watching airplane movies, we walked the boys to the hotel restaurant for dinner with their team, while we joined some fellow tourists gathered in the lobby. Mom and I were taking a special evening tour.

Mom skimmed over our itinerary. "We're in group C," she said, pointing to a sign.

It was a diverse bunch of about a dozen people—old, young, men, women, all different nationalities, shapes, and sizes. They flipped through brochures and unfolded maps.

A guy who looked a little older than me, wearing a shirt with the hotel's logo, came over. He was cute in a soccer player–like way: a few inches taller than me, with sun-bleached hair pulled away from his face and tied into a ponytail. "*Êtes-vous Américaine?* Are you American?" His accent was adorable and totally added to his cute factor.

"Yes. I'm Gwen Russell."

"Ah, someone was looking for you." He scanned the people in the hotel lobby and pointed to the familiar face of Brigitte Guyot. I'd met Brigitte in Pennsylvania when she and her family were living in the US for work that her dad was doing with my dad. We all hung out and became friends. She was like the big sister I never had, kind of a lot older—nine years. But then her dad's job moved them back to Paris.

He added, "You are going on the night tour to *la côte d'Albâtre*. It is . . . er . . . egg salad."

"Egg salad?"

"Um . . . how do you say? . . . *Formidable?*"

"Excellent?"

"*Oui.* Excellent! We say *excellent* too." He pointed to his name tag. "My name is Henri."

"You work here?"

"*Un peu* . . . er . . . a little, when I am not in school."

He turned me in the direction of a podium where a woman stood. "Listen carefully. She does not like it when people do not listen," he said. "I see you *plus tard* . . . er . . . later?"

"Yes," I said. I knew a little more than basic French, because I'd studied it in school and listened to some CDs, but mostly I'd learned it from Brigitte and her parents when they were in the US.

Brigitte was exactly like I remembered, except maybe a little older. Here's the deal: Brigitte was very nice but a little *unusual*.

Her brown hair was longer now, past her shoulders, and she was still very thin. She was tall—very tall, in fact. It seemed like her legs were longer than the rest of her body. Her glasses were square and thick. Her pants were pulled up too high, and she'd buttoned her shirt all the way up to her neck. Her unusual style actually made me smile, because the thing was, it suited her. She was kind of a quirky girl.

I hoped my outfit described me in a way that said, *Bonjour, Paris! Gwen Russell is in the house!* With three brothers, I was no expert in fashion, but I'd gotten sandals, hair clips, and lip gloss for this trip. Those were big advancements to my wardrobe.

Before I could talk to Brigitte, a small woman wearing a crisply starched uniform and a name tag identifying her as Madame LeBoeuf stood behind the tour guide podium. She glanced at the clipboard in her hand.

"Welcome to the Hôtel de Paris," she said with no

French accent at all. If anything, from her drawl, I'd have guessed she was from Alabama or Louisiana. "Tonight we will travel by bus to"—she paused at the French location—"*Atretat*, which is on the *coat de Albetross*." Man, she'd butchered *Étretat* on *la côte d'Albâtre*. She continued, "Where they launch the lanterns." She clapped twice to get the attention of a couple who was talking. She pointed to her ears and mouthed, *Listen up*. Henri wasn't kidding. She was serious about paying attention. "I will be joined tonight by my assistant." She waved to Henri, who was lifting a tapestry suitcase onto a cart.

Henri waved back, but his mouth gaped open for a second like this was a surprise to him. He forced a smile.

I was psyched to hear this because I wanted to talk more to Henri. He was cute, French, and seemed about my age. Plus, if he was as *sportif* as he looked, we had something in common.

I was good at most sports. Kind of by accident, really. You see, I'd been recruited for every backyard game my brothers played. Whoever was "stuck" with me on their team pressured me to be tougher, faster, and stronger. This meant that I made every team I tried out for. Now I was a three-sport girl: soccer, basketball, and lacrosse. It also meant that I often had black eyes, fat lips, and bruised legs. I'd had more broken fingers than anyone—boy or girl—in my school. I had a few girlfriends, but mostly I hung out with the boys.

Recently, I'd been trying to be more girly. My hair finally reached my shoulders, and my mom had bought me some trendy new clothes, which I'd brought with me.

Madame LeBoeuf continued, "You must stay with the group at all times. Raise your hands to ask questions. Speak slowly and clearly so that everyone can hear. Capeesh?" she snapped. Then she said, "If you require the facilities, now would be the time. We're leaving in five. That's *minutes*, people!" Her yelling definitely had a southern twang, proving there was nothing French at all about Madame LeBoeuf except her name. I used the translation app on my phone. *Le boeuf* was "beef." Kind of a perfect description of her too.

Everyone in group C scampered to the bathroom. But not me. This woman wouldn't scare me into going when I didn't have to. Instead I went to see Brigitte.

She hugged me, instantly transferring hair or fur or something strange and fuzzy from her shirt onto my new V-neck tee, which I'd tucked into capris.

"Gwen! The little sister I never had." I figured Brigitte was probably twenty-two years old now. "I am so glad you are both here," she said to Mom and me. "You are going to have a wonderful trip!"

"Are you coming on the night tour?" Mom asked her.

"Yes! I wouldn't miss it. I've lived here all my life and I've never been to *la côte d'Albâtre*," she said. "Besides, I want to hear all about every little thing going on in Pennsylvania."

Brigitte led us outside to the tour bus. I didn't get on the bus right away because I heard a familiar sound and started to wander toward it. A guitar.

There was a guy with a full beard, knit cap, wild hair, and sunglasses (at night), strumming and singing. The words were in English, something about running away. He stopped singing after lyrics about leaving worries behind. Brigitte nudged me to get on the bus. I did, but I wanted to come back later and hear more. In my town, no one hung out on the street and jammed like that.

Many seats were already taken, so all three of us couldn't sit together. Henri called me over to sit next to him. Yay!

Brigitte sat with Mom, and the two of them began to chatter.

I looked at the guitar guy through the window. "Is he there a lot?" I asked Henri.

"Every day. I see him at other places too. Do you like music?"

"I love it. My fave band is Shock Value. Do you know them?"

"Everyone knows Shock Value. They are very famous in France. One of the guys is French."

Together we said, "Winston!" He was the only French member of the band.

We shared a laugh. "They're big in America, too."

Henri asked, "You hear of the legs?"

"The legs?" I asked. Then I pointed to my legs. "Legs?"

"*Non. Non.* Not legs. It is like a story that I tell you and then you will tell another person . . . how you say? . . . Leg—"

"Legend?"

"*Oui!* Legend. You hear of the legend of the lanterns?"

I loved a good legend almost as much as I loved Shock Value. "Tell me."

"Parisians, they fly lanterns to the night sky at Étretat to welcome *l'été* . . . er . . . summer," Henri explained. "If you make a wish as you let your lantern"—he raised his hands over his head and then made a pushing motion—"out of your hands, it will come true."

And at those words, I knew exactly what my wish would be—an awesome week in Paris.

3

As the bus lurched down the streets of Paris, Henri asked me questions about my home and my school. I told him about my best friends, Lily McAllister and Addison Harper. And I asked him questions about France and his job. I thought it was pretty cool that he had a job at age fourteen. It was because friends of his parents owned the hotel.

"I play football," he said. "You call it soccer."

"I know it!" I said. "Me too!" I didn't add that I could play *football* football, too, and I knew how to box, wrestle, and lift kinda heavy weights. He didn't need to know that.

"I scored a winning goal today," he added.

"That's great! Congratulations."

"My friends were on the other team, and they are"—he made a growling face—"about me."

"They're mad?"

"*Oui.*"

"We call that sore losers," I said.

He nodded at the new term, but I didn't think it actually made sense to him.

Our chat was cut short because Beef, who was driving, called Henri in her loud, husky voice.

He hesitated to respond, like maybe she would forget.

She bellowed, "Henri!" again.

"Are you afraid of her?" I asked him.

We studied her. She had pulled a paper clip off a stack of stuff set on the armrest. She unfolded it and used an end to pick at her teeth.

"A little," he said as he reluctantly made his way up the aisle to the driver, where he listened to her.

While he was away, I took my notebook out of my drawstring backpack and crafted a few lyrics:

I met a boy in France.
He told me about a legend.

I planned to make a wish.
And let it sail away on a lantern.

In Étretat, we parked at a dirt field leading to the top of a rocky cliff.

Beef handed everyone in group C a paper lantern, and Henri followed her with candles and a lighter. There were a lot of other people launching lanterns off the edge of the cliff, and many other tour buses parked on the dirt.

I took a candle from Henri and stuck it on a poky thumbtack thingy inside the paper lantern. He lit it with his long lighter, careful not to burn the paper. I walked to the rope line that held people back from the edge of the cliff, and just like Henri had pantomimed, I pushed my lantern out toward the stars, letting it catch in the breeze. I watched it glide into the sky, which was blacker, with brighter stars, than in Pennsylvania. And I made a wish.

All the tourists in group C and hundreds of others threw their lanterns into the sky too. It was cool how the wind got under the lantern's paper edges and lifted it, as if the flame was hanging by a parachute. It looked like a swarm of slow-moving fireflies gliding in the blackness until the twinkle of the lanterns blended into the sparkle of the stars.

Henri stood next to me. "Did you wish?"

"Yup. And I'm very good at keeping secrets," I said.

"I will tell you mine. I cannot hold a secret."

I said, "No. Don't. Then it won't come true."

"It still might," Henri said. "No one knows."

"I'm still not telling you mine."

"D'accord," he said. "My wish was—"

I put my hand over his mouth. I don't think I'd ever actually touched a boy's lips, besides JTC's (that's my abbreviation for Josh, Topher, and Charlie). And when I covered their mouths with my hand, they would lick it. So gross. I moved my hand away before Henri could consider doing the same. "Don't tell me," I said.

He slouched like he'd given up.

I didn't know how long wishes usually took to come true, but these lantern ones seemed to take effect fast, because I was already having an awesome time in France with Henri.

Just then he blurted out, "I wish Les Bleus win the World Cup!" And he ran away.

Leave it to a boy to waste a wish on soccer!

I chased him and caught him easily.

"Mon Dieu, you are very fast for a girl."

I smacked him in the arm. He rubbed it. Maybe I'd run a little too fast and smacked him a little too hard. I could hit JTC as hard as I wanted, but I had to be more careful with other boys. "Now they're going to lose and it's going to be all your fault."

"They cannot lose." He rubbed his arm. "They are *formidable!*"

My phone vibrated in my pocket. This only happened when I got an important update in my Twister social media account. I looked at the notice flashing on my screen. It was from Shock Value. It said, *Concert: Shock Value has added one additional spot to their tour. PARIS. One night only.*

"Shock Value is coming to Paris!" I practically yelled in Henri's face.

My phone vibrated again. Another Twist from Shock Value. It said, *Paris concert SOLD OUT.*

"Holy cow! It's already sold out," I said.

"A cow?" Henri asked.

"Sorry. It's just an expression in English. Kinda like 'oh my gosh!'"

The phone vibrated for a third time. *What now?* It said, *Shock Value ticket contest! Follow the hunt around Paris and win tickets to the special one-night engagement in Paris.*

"Check this out." I showed Henri.

"Cow!" he yelled.

I looked at my watch. We'd only been here for fifteen

minutes, but we had to get on this contest, like, double pronto.

"We've got to get Beef to get this train moving."

"Train?"

"Bus. Small van, actually," I clarified. "We've gotta start looking for those tickets!"

Henri waved me ahead. "Ladies first."

Yeah, my wish had already started.

Beef leaned against the van, going with the paper clip again. "Hi there," I said. *"Bonjour,"* I added. "I kinda have to get back to the hotel, like now."

"What's the rush?"

"You see, there's this band; I really like them. They're called Shock Value."

"Who doesn't love Shock Value?" she asked. "I love that one they call Clay. Too bad he quit. Anyway, they're still great." She looked at her watch. "But we're on a schedule, and this bus don't move until it's time."

"Right. I totes agree with you on Clay, and schedules. I love to be on schedule," I said. "But the band, Shock Value, they're having this contest for tickets to a one-night concert they just added right here in Paris. And—"

Beef dropped her paper clip, jumped into the bus, and started honking the horn. She took her phone out and brushed her finger across the screen, scanning

18

pages. She honked again and again. Then she stood on the ground next to the hotel bus with a megaphone. "Let's go, people! We're cutting this excursion short because musical history is being made. Shock Value has just announced a new concert and I wanna get tickets. Let's go."

Everyone hustled to the bus as directed. I grabbed Henri's shirt and tugged him to run faster.

We sat near Mom and Brigitte and waited for the last few people to get on the bus. "Let's go, Wheels," Beef called to a man in a wheelchair, who was taking longer than everyone else. He was hardly secured when she threw the bus into drive and skidded through the gravel parking area.

Now she wore a headset thing that dangled a microphone in front of her mouth. "For those of you less adept at social media than *moi*, I'll fill you in on the four-one-one Twisted from Twister.com." She aggressively navigated around other cars pulling out of the lot. I had to hold tight to the seat in front of me so that I didn't fly into the aisle. "Shock Value has announced a one-night concert in Paris and a contest for tickets."

"They haven't been quite the same since Clay Bright left," Brigitte said.

"Who's that?" Mom asked.

Brigitte explained, "Clay was their guitarist and he wrote their music. One day he quit—"

I interrupted. "He didn't just quit. He disappeared. Like, totally off the grid. Even his bandmates, who were also his best friends, claim they've never heard from him."

Brigitte nodded and continued, "The band didn't replace him. They're still the most awesome band around. It's impossible to get tickets."

"Who's talking?" Beef barked. "Listen up, people, or you'll miss the critical deets. The show sold out in four minutes, a new record. But front-row tickets and back-stage passes are being given away to three lucky people who follow a trail of clues that the band has left around Paris. If you haven't noticed, I know pretty much every-thing about Paris, so those babies are as good as mine."

"Mom, we absolutely have *got* to get tickets," I said. "I'm in Paris; they're in Paris. It's like it was meant to be." I didn't wait for a response.

"Where's the first clue?" I called to Beef.

"Seems like *someone* wasn't paying attention to the instructions before we left the hotel," she snapped. "The world would be total chaos if people just called out any-time they wanted."

I raised my hand, but she didn't call on me.

"The first clue will be released at nine tomorrow

morning. For those of us participating in this treasure hunt, we have to prepare before getting a solid eight hours of shut-eye," Beef said. "I know you all want to be on my team. But, there are only three tickets, and since we don't have time for a formal application process, I'll pick."

Beef was scary and mean and picked her teeth with a paper clip, but she was a tour guide. Who would know more about Paris? *Please pick me!*

She looked at the man in the wheelchair. "Wheels, there's something I like about you. You're with me, but we're gonna have to add a little horsepower to your motor. I know a guy."

The man in the wheelchair didn't seem to understand any of this. Henri leaned over and whispered in his ear. Wheels clapped when Henri finished; apparently he was a fan. But, really, *I* was their biggest fan, so I should totally get those tickets.

The man in the wheelchair pointed to a young lady with a stethoscope dangling around her neck. "Fine," Beef said. "She can come too."

Looked like Gwen Russell wouldn't be hunting on Team Beef.

My mom whispered very softly, "I don't want to get in trouble for talking, but do you think we should try to get tickets?"

"Really? Are you serious?" Shock Value—Alec, Winston, and Glen—occupied every inch of every wall in my bedroom. I knew every word to every song. "YES! I think we should try to get the tickets!"

"Let's do it!" she said. "The boys are leaving at nine o'clock tomorrow morning for lacrosse, so we're free."

I couldn't believe it. Less than a day in Paris, and I was in the running for tickets for Shock Value—AND I was going to see the city in the coolest way possible!

And Mom was actually on board with this plan! I didn't know who had swapped my mom for this totally cool lady, but I was pretty sure it had something to do with a lantern and a certain wish.

4

The lacrosse bus was parked in front of the hotel ahead of schedule. The driver put up his hand and stopped JTC from getting on the bus. He came over to talk to my mom. *"Bonjour, madame. Je crois qu'il y a un problème."*

Mom didn't speak French, but she understood "problem."

"Les garçons—et un parent," the bus driver said, trying to explain.

Mom held up her palm. She walked away and came back with Brigitte, who'd been waiting in the lobby when we got off the elevator. Brigitte began speaking to the driver in French. Then she said to Mom, "The boys, they need a parent."

"Oh. Oh my."

Brigitte explained this to the bus driver, who replied something in very fast French.

Brigitte said, "Yes, they can go with the team, but they must have a parent with them."

Mom looked at me. "I guess you'll have to come too. I'm so sorry we can't do the treasure hunt. Maybe we can still buy regular tickets."

"It's sold out, remember?" I said. "I'm not going to another one of their tournaments. I could do that in Pennsylvania. We're in Paris!"

I thought of a few lines of lyrics:

Wishing on paper lanterns does NOT work.
Don't let the French tell you it's true.
Because it's not.
It's not.

Topher called out the bus window, "Yo, Mrs. Russell, you're holding up the team!"

She motioned that she needed one minute. As I like to say, her *one minute* finger.

While she thought, Charlie yelled out, "Paris is sweet, huh, Gwenny?"

Right now I hated JTC. They always ruined everything.

"Well, you can't just hang out alone at a hotel in a foreign country," Mom said.

"I won't be alone. I'll be with Brigitte." I grabbed Brigitte's hand. She looked at me in surprise.

Mom studied the two of us.

"It is a good idea," Brigitte said. "I will take care of her like she was my very own sister. You go to the game. It is fine."

"Are you sure?" Mom asked her. "Don't you have to work?"

"No problem." She smiled. "She can go with me to care for the pets."

"What pets?" Mom asked.

"My job—a business, actually. I care for people's pets while they are out of town. It is called 'Boutique Brigitte—Pour les Petits Animaux.'"

"You do? I love pets," I said.

"*Oui.* I have a minivan and everything!" Brigitte explained. "And we can look for the clues. But work comes first." She shooed Mom away. "Go. *Allez!*" Brigitte had just climbed, like, four notches on the cool scale.

"Okay," Mom said. "But, Gwen, seriously, Brigitte's job is her priority."

"I get it," I said. "We can do both." Brigitte had lived in Paris her whole life, except for the two years in Pennsylvania, and she had a minivan. I still had a shot at those tickets.

Mom took out her wallet and gave me money.

Josh called out, "What's that for? I want money!"

Charlie added, "What's she doing that she needs cash?"

I said, "I'm getting front-row seats to Shock Value."

"Yeah, right," Topher said. "That'll happen right after Charlie can make a shot from outside the box."

Charlie punched Topher, and a wrestling match ensued.

"I have to go," Mom said. "Behave. Brigitte has a job to do, and *that* comes before the Shock Value tickets, understand? Please try to be low maintenance."

"I can totally do low maintenance," I said.

Mom got on the bus.

Charlie called out the window to Brigitte, "It's okay if you lose her."

I stuck out my tongue.

The bus pulled away, and Brigitte said to me, "I won't lose you. Just stay close. Be like my . . . how do you say? . . . shadow."

"Got it."

Henri pushed an empty luggage cart to the curb. "Is everything *bien*?"

I thought about telling him that the whole wishing-on-a-lantern thing was a charade, but when he flashed me this super-cute smile, I forgot what I was going to say. "What are you up to?" I asked.

"Up?" He looked at the sky.

"I meant, what are you doing?"

"I have to shave the courtyard."

"What?"

"You know"—he made a scissoring motion with his fingers—"give the plants a haircut."

"Oh. Trim the hedges."

"Right." He smiled. "Are you looking for the tickets?"

"Yeah. With Brigitte," I said. "Will I see you tonight?"

"If I am still shaving . . . er . . . trimming, maybe we can get *le gâteau*."

I knew *le gâteau* was cake. "Deal!"

Cake with a cute French soccer player? Potential front-row tickets to Shock Value? Maybe those French legends really were true.

5

At exactly nine a.m. the lacrosse bus full of boys and parents pulled out. Brigitte and I leaned over my smartphone and looked at the Shock Value site on Twister.com, and . . . *wait for it . . .* there it was:

> You cannot make me laugh nor cry. If you
> touch me, you will find that I'm cold. I
> cannot embrace anyone to get warm. People
> travel far and wide to see me, and despite
> my flaws, they're awed by my beauty.

"What do you think it is?" I asked Brigitte.

"I do not know," she said.

"You're from Paris. How can you not know?"

"I do not do the tourist things. I run a pet-sitting business." She glanced at her watch. "In fact, we need to get to little Fifi before she leaves a little pee-pee on her apartment floor."

"Now?"

"Yes. I have a schedule," she said. "I will go to get the petmobile. That lacrosse bus took my usual spot. The petmobile gets priority parking at most hotels and apartments," Brigitte said. "You stay right here and try to figure out that clue!"

"Okay." *Petmobile?* I went back inside to a rack of booklets and brochures and grabbed everything I could. Maybe there was something in here that would help. A white paper was taped to Beef's podium; it said, *All tours will be led by Étienne.* Seemed she was serious about this contest.

Then I typed a search into my phone using the words of the clue. I tried different combinations, but just got junk.

Beef whizzed out of the hotel, standing on the back of the wheelchair like she was on a carnival ride. She zipped along the sidewalk to the Hôtel de Paris bus, whose ramp was already lowered. The wheelchair flew into the bus like a race car. Apparently, her guy had come through with the horsepower. A third person, the young woman who still had a stethoscope, followed them, much more slowly since she was weighed down with a gigantic hiking backpack. There were three sleeping bags affixed above and below the main pack. Pots and pans hung on the bottom and jingled as she waddled toward the bus. She also had a big duffel bag in each hand.

Wow, Beef was prepared with a capital *P*. How were we going to compete with her? She was focused only on the hunt, while we had to run a pet business at the same time.

"Wait, Professor Camponi," the woman called. "It's time for your medicine."

"Get in!" Beef called to her, already pulling away. The woman had to jog and jump into the moving bus.

Through the windows I saw the woman hand Professor Camponi—which was a much better name than Wheels—a bottle of water and a pill. Then the bus peeled out with a screech and she fell into a seat.

Where was Brigitte? If we hurried, we might be able to follow them. I looked down the boulevard to the right and left, but didn't see Brigitte, and now I'd also lost sight of Beef. Following was no longer a possibility.

I mumbled the words of the clue. Then from behind me I heard someone singing the same lines, as though they were lyrics. I recognized the voice. It was the guitar player with the beard, knit cap, and sunglasses.

He stopped singing. "Good stuff," he said.

"How do you know those words?"

"I have Twister.com too." He patted the front pocket of his worn jeans, indicating that even a sidewalk guitarist had a smartphone.

"Do you know what it means?"

"Of course," he said. "It's one of my favorite things to see in Paris. I may be American, but I've been all around this city. I'll help you out."

6

I waited for Brigitte on the sidewalk. Suddenly I heard a really loud rumble. The contraption that drove up the boulevard to pick me up was an unbelievable sight. I blinked, but it was still there.

It was a white minivan covered with black paw prints, like a gang of cats and dogs had stepped in black paint and run all over it. Stuck to the front was a basketball, colored to look like a pink cat nose with wire whiskers sticking out the sides, and on the roof were two pointy ears. The van stopped in front of the hotel and it actually barked! Yes, barked.

I had a whole new appreciation for my mom's old minivan.

I hustled into the passenger seat and buried my head in my hands. "To the Louvre," I said.

"You figured it out?" Brigitte asked. She checked her seat belt and adjusted her rearview mirror, then her side mirror.

"Yes. Come on. We've gotta go. Beef left in a hurry."

"Beef?" Brigitte asked.

"Sorry. I meant Madame LeBoeuf."

"Ha! *Non*, I like Beef better," Brigitte said. "Okay. Here we go." She adjusted the side mirror again, put on her directional blinker, and rolled down her window to point to the road she was easing out onto.

I looked at the cars around us. "You look all clear," I said as a hint to speed up.

"To the Louvre," she said, but she didn't drive any faster.

Did she not realize what was at stake?

She continued at the pace of a turtle with three broken legs all the way to a parking spot near the Louvre. We dashed out. Brigitte managed to run faster than she drove. Through three giant arches I caught my first glimpse of the great glass pyramid of . . . *wait for it* . . . the Louvre! Even though I was in a hurry, I had to stop for just a second in the huge courtyard to marvel at where I was standing. The pyramid was framed on three sides by a breathtaking building.

"It's like a palace," I said to Brigitte.

"It actually *was* a palace for hundreds of years until Louis the Fourteenth moved the king's home to Versailles. Then it became the place to keep the royal art collections. As kings grew the art collection, the building's size grew too," Brigitte said.

I looked at her with surprise at this little history lesson, because she'd seemed to know nothing when she'd looked at the first clue. "What?" she said. "I am French. Of course I know about the Louvre."

"Well, it is amazing."

"Masterpiece," she said. "It is large and most magnificent."

"It is." I wanted to stay longer—I could've spent the entire week in this one spot—but the hunt . . . the hunt. We had to move quickly. We made our way to the ticketing lines and were immediately sucked into crowds of tourists and what looked like other Shock Value hunters.

"*Mon Dieu!*" Brigitte said. "This line will take all day."

"Isn't there a shortcut?"

"It looks like Beef has already found one." She craned her neck to indicate Beef riding on the back of the wheelchair to the spot where people needing extra assistance didn't have to wait in line. The nurse lady, whose backpack had been replaced with Beef's fanny pack, held a clipboard and ran to keep up with the speeding chair. Beef seemed to have thought this all out.

"What are we gonna do?" I asked.

"I have an idea of my own."

Brigitte struck me as a person who followed the rules exactly, so I was skeptical. "You do?"

She reached into her back pocket and pulled out a little black book that said ADRESSES on it.

"What's that?" I asked.

"It's the list of clients for Boutique Brigitte—Pour les Petits Animaux."

"How is that going to help?"

"People love their pets. . . ."

"Sure."

"They love people who take good care of their pets. . . ."

"Okay."

"And they are willing to help them. . . ."

"All right."

"One of them works here," Brigitte said.

Now I caught on. That little black book was like a list of secret helpers. I didn't know how many clients Brigitte had, but I hoped she had one who could help us with every clue. *That* was something Beef didn't have.

Brigitte dialed her phone. *"Bonjour, Monsieur Willmott, c'est Brigitte,"* she said. Then she explained that we were on the hunt for Shock Value tickets and needed to beat the crowd to the clue—Monsieur Willmott must have interrupted her, because she suddenly stopped talking and listened. Her expression was serious like it wasn't good news, but then she grinned.

"Merci! Merci beaucoup!" She hung up. "We're in!"

"We are? How?"

"Follow me. We need to make a little . . . how do you say? . . . delivery."

"Delivery?" I followed Brigitte back to the petmobile. "We don't have time to make a delivery."

She threw open the back door and tossed an empty brown cardboard box out. She scribbled over the label that said SHAMPOOING POUR CHIEN and wrote the address for the Louvre. And added *Attention: M. Willmott.* Then she climbed in the back of the van and took out two black lab coats. They were covered with pet fur.

"This is the closest thing we have to a delivery uniform." Then she put a baseball hat on each of our heads.

There was no way this was gonna pass as a delivery company uniform. She said, "Make a business face, like this." She pushed her smile down, squinted her eyes a

36

bit, and forced wrinkles onto her forehead. Then, in a lower voice, she said, "Delivery for"—she glanced at the box—"Monsieur Willmott." When she was done with the little charade, she laughed with a snort.

She was actually a pretty good actress, but I didn't believe the act would work, especially if she let a snort slip out.

She closed up the petmobile and ran ahead with the empty box. "What will you say to Shock Value when you meet them?"

I hadn't had time to think about it. What would I say? Before I could answer, we were at a door that said LIVRAISONS. I knew that meant "deliveries." Brigitte pushed a button. A security guard answered the door.

She wasn't gonna fool this guy.

He looked at the box, glanced up at a security camera that probably made sure no one other than real delivery people came through the door, and asked, "*Livraison?*"

Brigitte nodded.

He winked, moved aside, and let us pass.

We were in!

The security man took the box and directed us down a corridor with another wink. Maybe he could tell I was American, because he directed us in English, "Go that way and turn right."

Brigitte gave him a tiny hug and said, "*Merci,* Monsieur Willmott."

We raced down a small hall and turned right as he'd said. When we emerged into the museum, we were among a smaller crowd heading up the stairs to admire the famous statue of Venus de Milo:

> *You cannot make me laugh nor cry. If you*
> *touch me, you will find that I'm cold. I*
> *cannot embrace anyone to get warm. People*
> *travel far and wide to see me, and despite*
> *my flaws, they're awed by my beauty.*

Venus de Milo couldn't embrace anyone, because she didn't have arms. They'd been broken off and lost somewhere in time. Clearly, the guitarist in the knit cap wasn't the only one who knew this answer, because a bunch of what had to be other fans crowded around a girl wearing a royal blue Shock Value shirt, but I just stared at the statue. She was so pretty, chiseled perfectly from marble, yet she looked like she'd be soft if I touched her. She had been sculpted in the likeness of Aphrodite, the Greek goddess of love and beauty. And she really was beautiful.

I snapped back to the contest and realized that the girl in the Shock Value shirt was explaining the next part. "The first ten teams get the next clue. Go stand on a number." On the floor sat round rubber pads, each with a number—one through ten. The spaces numbered one through four were occupied. I jumped for number five only to be beaten by a girl who had pierced everything on her face. I didn't want to mess with her. As I stepped on number six, the tip of my new sneaker squished as it was run over by a speeding wheelchair.

"Ow!" I yelped.

"Too slow," said Beef.

"I was here first," I said.

Beef, Professor Camponi, and the nurse lady squarely occupied space number six. I suppressed the urge to clobber them like I would if Charlie blocked the last piece of pizza from me, but Brigitte calmly pulled my furry lab coat to space number seven.

"All ten people get a clue," she said. "Space number seven is okay."

"It was the principle," I said. "She is pushy and bossy and I don't like her."

Once all ten spaces were filled, the Shock Value representative handed each team a small royal blue gift bag. "Welcome to the contest," she said. "You are the ten teams competing for the three front-row seats and passes to Shock Value's special one-night engagement in Paris this Friday. You'll get to see all the backstage action during the concert and maybe catch a glimpse of Winston, Glen, and Alec themselves."

Glimpse?

I wanted more than a glimpse. I wanted to meet the band.

"A Shock Value rep will meet you at each clue's location to give you the next bag. The first team to successfully follow all the clues and make it to the end of the trail will get the epic treasure!"

Everyone on the ten teams clapped.

She continued, "So, good luck. The next clue is in that bag. Make sure you give me your names and cell phone numbers; then you can take the bag and go!"

Everyone opened their bags except Beef, who tossed a business card to the Shock Value rep, fired up the chair, hopped on the back, and whizzed away from the beautiful Venus de Milo.

7

Brigitte bent to tie her shoe. "What is it?" she asked me
without looking at the clue.

I held it up. "It's like a little model of a building." I
looked at it. "Not a building, really, because there aren't
windows . . . it's like a monument, maybe. We have one in
Washington DC called the Washington Monument. There
are words on the side." I turned it. "'It's time to fly' is etched
along the side." I put the little building in my pocket.

Brigitte stood back up. "It's time to fly," she repeated,
and thought.

"Does that mean anything to you?"

"Nope. Nothing." She looked at her watch. "We'll think about it on the way."

"Where?"

"Fifi. Pee-pee. Remember?"

I didn't like the idea of disrupting our search now, but since we didn't know where to go next, "To Fifi," I agreed.

On the short drive over, we brainstormed different ideas. "It's time to fly." I put it in Google, but didn't get anything useful. "These are harder than I thought," I complained.

"Which one is your favorite?" Brigitte asked me.

"Which what?"

"Band member. Alec, Winston, or Glen?" she asked.

"I can only pick one?"

"Only one."

"Winston," I said. "How about you?"

"Alec."

"Why Alec?"

"He is British! I love the Brits!" she said. "Why Winston?"

"He's the cutest. And the youngest," I said. "And I love his French accent."

The Shock Value members were a mix of ages. From youngest to oldest there was Winston (16), Alec (20), and Glen (26). Clay was thirty when he disappeared. The two oldest, Glen and Clay, were also the two Americans of the band.

Shock Value won a big TV talent contest three years ago and came out with an awesome (with a capital *A*) song. When Clay disappeared a year ago, they stopped recording and touring. Everyone was surprised they didn't replace him. Then a few months ago they released a new album without Clay. The music sounded a little different, but it was still fab.

Brigitte drove past a huge church. I could see the giant spires and what looked like little monsters etched into the sides. Based on pictures, I could tell it was Notre Dame Cathedral.

"Look at those scary statues," I said.

"We call them *gargouilles*," Brigitte said.

"Sounds exactly like what we call them, gargoyles," I said. "Isn't it convenient when French and English words are the same, or almost the same?"

"Oui." Brigitte giggled, and we made a list of words that were the same in both languages: *ski, bizarre, important, zoo, menu, garage*. And, most important to me, *boutique*!

"We're here." Brigitte pulled up in front of a four-story apartment building with beautiful iron balconies that looked *très chic*. A doorman came to the petmobile and opened my door for me. *"Bonjour,"* he said in a husky voice, *"Brigitte pour les petits animaux.* Fifi is waiting for you."

"Merci, Philippe," Brigitte said. "We won't be long. We're on the hunt for those Shock Value tickets. Did you hear about the contest?"

"Of course!" Philippe said. "If I had more time, I would try it myself."

"Ask him if he knows what the clue means," I whispered to her.

"Ah, Philippe, do you know what 'It's time to fly' means? It's our clue."

He rubbed his chin. "Time to fly . . . time to fly . . . *l'aéroport?* The time of a flight?"

Hmmm. That sounded possible.

"Maybe," she said. *"Merci."* I followed her to the elevator, which was like none I'd ever seen. We stood on a platform, and Brigitte pulled a caged wall down in front of us. The elevator rattled as it brought us to the fourth floor. I held on to the waist-high railing for support. "Orly is one of our airports," Brigitte said. "Very big."

"It may not be a big airport."

"True." She lifted the cage and walked to the first door in the hallway. She pulled a gigantic key ring out of her lab coat pocket. The rounded end of each key had a rubber cap. And each cap had a name written in slim black letters. She found Fifi's key.

A white, puffy, fluffy, yappy pup ran to the door. When it tried to stop, it slid across the hardwood floor until it hit the wall with a little thud. Fifi didn't seem to mind. She redirected toward us and yapped more.

"*Bonjour*, Fifi!" Brigitte talked in a baby voice. She pulled a leash out of another lab coat pocket and put it on the pooch. "*Comment vas-tu? Est-ce que tu étais une bonne chienne? Allons-y,*" she said to Fifi.

We went back down in the elevator and walked down the boulevard, which was lined with many more buildings like Fifi's. We turned a corner at La Boulangerie Moderne, a French bakery whose outside walls were painted brick red and trimmed in gold paint. The red-and-gold awning was decorated with the name and phone number in beautiful cursive.

With the smell of croissants in our wake I saw a brilliant building that made me think I was suddenly in Italy, not France. "Wow! What's that?"

"The Panthéon."

"What is it?"

"It is one of my favorite places in Paris. Actually, it wouldn't be fair to all of my other favorite places if they heard me say that. But I like it a lot." She lowered her voice. "It holds the remains of important people. You know what I mean by *remains*?"

"Like, the bodies?" I asked.

"Corpses," she added to make the idea of it more gruesome.

"Maybe we won't go in there," I said.

She perked back up. "Besides the remains, it is a very beautiful mausoleum. And I love the story of why it was built."

"I like a good story," I said. "Tell me."

"King Louis the Fifteenth was very sick. He made a vow to God himself. He said that if he recovered, he would replace the ruined church that used to be here with a magnificent building. Then, he did recover! And built this. It looks over all of Paris." As quickly as she'd given me the brief history lesson, she refocused on Fifi, baby-talking more in French. She was more interested in the dog than in the incredible historic building in front of us. Maybe she was used to walking around seeing ancient stuff and buildings like this, but I wasn't.

While I thought the Panthéon was beautiful and I wanted to learn about it, it didn't have anything to do with "it's time to fly."

"Wait," I said. "Gargoyles fly, don't they? Maybe 'a

time to fly' is sending us to a gargoyle in Paris." I googled "gargoyles in Paris." Hmm. "There are hundreds across the city. Way too many to check out."

"Maybe it's about telling time. Like a watch," she said.

"Of course!" I yelled. "That's brilliant. Is there a famous clock tower?"

"There is! Gare de Lyon, but maybe that is too . . . like, too easy . . ."

"Obvious?" I asked.

"Right. Obvious," she said. "I was thinking that Paris is home to the most famous watches."

"Is there a factory?"

"No, a store," she said. "Cartier!"

8

"What about Fifi?" Brigitte asked.

"This is a race, Brigitte! Bring her. Hurry!"

We ran to the petmobile. For having such little legs, Fifi could run fast.

Brigitte retrieved a gadget from the back of the van and strapped it into the backseat. She set Fifi into the thing, which was very like an infant car seat, secured a harness over Fifi's fluffy paws, and clicked the seat belt. Fifi could only be more protected if we wrapped her in bubble wrap, but I didn't mention that because it wouldn't have surprised me if Brigitte had bubble wrap in one of her pockets. Brigitte got in the front and ever so cautiously pulled out into traffic, checking her mirrors over and over, rolling the window down, and pointing to the spot she was moving to.

I thought about explaining the part about the race again.

She drove with both hands firmly clenched around the steering wheel, and she leaned in close to the windshield. I didn't want to break her concentration and I didn't want to make her angry. After all, the only reason I was able to participate at all was because she'd agreed to be my "babysitter." And it was pretty awesome that she had a car and was interested in this hunt too. If she quit on me, I'd be in a major jam.

Even at our snail's pace it didn't take long to arrive at the Cartier store in la place Vendôme. Brigitte parallel parked right in front of the Cartier store. When she backed up the petmobile, it made a *Beep! Beep! Beep!* that attracted even more attention than the average minivan dressed like a cat-dog.

There was no sign of the Hôtel de Paris bus. Either Beef had already been here or, hopefully, we'd beat her. I had a good feeling about this place. Beef had probably gone straight to the obvious clock tower.

I glanced around for some sign of a Shock Value rep;
I didn't see one. Maybe she wouldn't be dressed in a blue
shirt at each location. Maybe she'd even be hidden or
undercover, like as a store employee.

Each of the windows was decorated with white
lights and displays of watches on black velvet wrists. A
half-moon awning covered every window, with the word
Cartier written across it in posh script.

In a word, this place looked *fancy*.

Brigitte examined me, and then herself. "Wait. We
can't go in like this." She opened the back of the petmobile.
She scavenged around and found a purple sequined beret,
which she put on my head, slightly off to the side. If you
looked at it closely, you could tell that it had two ear holes.
Then she took three leashes, braided them together, and
wrapped them around my neck like some *nouveau* fashion statement. She took her lab coat and tied it over her
shoulders like a cape of sorts, unbuckled Fifi, and tucked
her under her arm like an accessory. If you didn't look *too*
closely, we could possibly pass for two chic gals shopping
for an upscale watch. For a last touch I grabbed a pair of
postage stamp–shaped sunglasses with wire frames from
the bottom of a box of junk. I wiped off the smudges that
were probably from the last dog who'd worn them, and set
them on the end of my nose.

We marched into the exquisite watch store like we totally belonged. I walked to the counter, glancing down at the bejeweled watches.

"Can I help you?" a man in a pin-striped suit asked. He eyed me with a mix of curiosity and disgust.

I peered right over the top of the sunglasses looking for the girl from Shock Value. She was nowhere. Maybe this guy worked for the band. I whispered, "It's time to fly," like it was a secret password, and slid the glasses back over my eyes to conceal my true identity.

He paused, maybe considering if I was worthy of it. Then he asked, *"Pardon?"*

I repeated, in case he was just checking to see if he heard it right, "It's time to fly."

He exhaled as though I'd annoyed him. "Can I help you or not, *mademoiselle?*"

I guess not.

I whispered to Brigitte, "I don't think this is the place."

She nodded, and like a customer who couldn't find anything suitable, she stuck her nose into the air, tightened her grip on her white fluffy dog, and marched out.

If Brigitte didn't succeed as Paris's premier pet sitter, she might seriously have a future in acting. As Brigitte buckled Fifi up, I said, "That was embarrassing."

"Nah. We'll never see them again. Besides, I always

figure they have seen some person more odd than me," she said. She put the van in drive and focused on the road. "Where are we going?"

"I can't help but think that I've seen that monument in one of my tour books. Let's go back to the hotel and I'll look it up."

"*Bien.* That is not far."

Again, Brigitte drove like a snail on a leisurely ride. I was glad she was a safe driver, but it bugged me that she didn't realize that we were in a hurry! It seemed like every car was flying by us. Some honked. Brigitte just waved at them and smiled.

I ran into the Hôtel de Paris and lingered for just one extra second in the lobby to see if Henri was working, but I didn't see him. I was about to race up the center staircase when I heard, *"Salut!"* I turned to see Henri standing in the fireplace, covered with soot. "How are you?" he asked.

"Great! What are you up to?"

He looked up for only a second, then remembered that I didn't mean "up." "I am dusting the fire chimney." He looked at my hand. "What is that?"

"It's a clue for the Shock Value treasure hunt. It's some monument with a message: 'It's time to fly.' We're trying to figure out what it means. I'm going up to get a book to see what it is."

"It is not a monument."

"It's not?" I asked.

"*Non*. It is an *obélisque*."

"What's that?"

"It's tall and stone. When the sun shines, it makes a dark mark on the ground."

"Like a shadow?"

"Right. That is it! A shadow to tell the time. Like before clocks."

"Like a sundial?" I asked. "Or an obelisk?"

"*Oui*, but a very big one," he said. "It is in la place de la Concorde."

"Do you know how to get there?" I asked.

"*Bien sûr*." Of course.

9

I dragged Henri to the petmobile, careful not to pull too hard or run too fast. Brigitte was letting Fifi pee-pee.

"It's time to fly," I said to Brigitte. "Henri knows what this is and where to go." I opened the back door for Henri, picked up Fifi, and put her on his lap.

"You are all dirty," Brigitte said to Henri. Was she worried he might soil white fluffy Fifi? "Buckle Fifi up, please," she asked him.

He messed around with the seat belt and the dog harness, and the whole time Fifi licked him on the face.

He didn't appear to enjoy the bath, but it washed off some of the ash.

Henri directed Brigitte to la place de la Concorde.

"I know where it is. I just can't believe I didn't recognize it. I guess because it was so small," Brigitte said.

"You drive very slow," Henri said to her.

"I am careful and safe."

"It feels very slow," he said again.

"Safe," she corrected.

I think he might have said "slow" again under his breath.

"*Là-bas!*" Henri shouted. Fifi barked.

There it was. A tall obelisk surrounded by an oval boulevard. Two magnificent fountains occupied where the twelve o'clock and six o'clock spaces would be if this whole oval were, in fact, a huge sundial. I saw a royal blue shirt in the distance. "Pull over. I'll run and get the next clue."

Brigitte honked the barking horn to get people to move out of the way. Henri and I jumped out before the petmobile came to a complete stop and ran across the cobblestone street that became a sidewalk.

The Shock Value rep stood at the base of the obelisk. "Hi there," she said. "Good to see you." She handed us a royal blue bag. "Good luck."

A woman holding a microphone, followed by a

cameraman, walked over to me. *"Bonjour,"* she said. "I'm Murielle duPluie, covering music news. Can we ask you a few questions?"

Did they want to interview us because we were in first place? We must be pretty far in the lead for this to be news. OMG, I was going to make the French news! *How cool is that?* "Okay," I said.

"What is your name and where are you from?"

"I'm Gwen Russell, from the US—U-S-A!—and I'm Shock Value's number one fan."

"Can you tell me, Gwen Russell from the USA, how does it feel to be in last place?"

Last place? "Well, I wasn't . . . I didn't . . . ," I sputtered. I was going to be a laughingstock on the French news. I was representing my country, not unlike an Olympic athlete, and I was letting all Americans down.

Murielle duPluie asked, "What is your strategy to get back in the game?"

"Umm . . . we need to find the clues faster, I think."

"And how do you plan to do that?"

"We, umm . . . we . . ."

Henri came into the frame of the camera and said, "She has me on her team. I am Henri and I am *formidable* at puzzles and soccer. I am the team's . . . how would you say? . . . A missile that no one knows about."

"A secret weapon?" Murielle duPluie asked.

"*Exactement!* We will see you, Madame duPluie, at the next clue, and we will not be last," Henri said.

He'd saved it. Maybe I wouldn't be a total embarrassment to my country. But now the pressure was really on. We'd made a public declaration not to be last. All eyes were on us.

Henri and I were walking toward the petmobile with our royal blue bag when two people blocked our way.

"Ha! ha! *Bonjour*, Henri," said a guy wearing a Paris Football Club shirt. "Your car barks."

"It is a petmobile," Henri clarified defensively. "*Bonjour*, Sabine," he said to the girl with him. It was the girl with the piercings who had occupied space number five at Venus de Milo.

She asked me, "Is Henri on your pet team?"

"I am helping them," Henri answered for me.

Soccer Guy said to me, "You don't have a chance." He laughed. To Henri he said, "You got lucky at the game, but it won't happen again. Not at soccer and not at this contest." Then he made a mean bark.

A car screeched to a halt. Sabine and the guy laughed and barked as they got into it.

Another boy in a soccer shirt was driving. He yelled out the window, "*Salut*, Henri! How does it feel to be in last place?"

They drove away with squealing tires.

"Who are they?" I asked.

"They are the . . . what did you call them? . . . sore losers," he explained. "Sabine and I, we sort of . . . how do you say? . . . go together?"

"Date?"

"Dated. But now she dates Jean-Luc. The other guy, the driver, is Robert."

"And you don't like them?" I asked.

"No. They are very mad that my soccer team is good."

"They sound like jerks," I said. "We have a saying in the US when we compete with people like them. Game on!"

"I like that." He repeated, "Game on!"

10

We got in the petmobile and Fifi instantly licked Henri's face like he'd been gone forever and she'd missed him terribly. He didn't smile as he tried to wipe his face.

"What was that all about?" Brigitte asked.

"We're in last place," I said. "That was a reporter who wanted an interview."

"Did you mention Boutique Brigitte? It would be good for business for that to be on the news," she said.

"Um, it didn't come up," I said.

"What is in the bag?" Brigitte asked.

Henri asked, "If the game is on, am I in the game? Like, on the team?"

"I don't think my mom would mind. Besides, how can she actually be on the team when she isn't here to help?" I asked.

"I am here to help," Henri confirmed.

"What about your job?" I asked him.

"It is like bending rubber."

"What?"

"My boss, he is friends with my parents and he bends for me."

"You mean it's flexible."

"*Oui*. And bendable."

"Then it's official. We three will be a team," I said.

Henri gave me a high five. "*Formidable!* Now, what is in *le sac*?"

I opened the bag and took out a key hanging by a royal blue ribbon.

"*Une clé*," Henri said.

"I wonder what it goes to," I said. "A door somewhere? A secret room? And inside we'll find the next clue."

"Not a hotel," Henri said. "They use cards."

"True," I said. "Do you think this is the last clue and Shock Value will actually be there? Like, we'll open the door and they'll *pop out*?"

"Or, maybe the key is to a box or a locker," Brigitte said.

"The band cannot fit in a box or locker," Henri said.

"Where would we find lockers?" I asked. "Train stations?"

"*Oui*, and bus stations and airports. But the lockers at bus stations and *metro* stations are like . . ." He pantomimed twisting right and left with his fingers. "And numbers."

"A combination?"

"*Oui*. Combination," Henri confirmed.

"Or you put in money and then take an orange key out of the locker. The key has a number, which matches the locker," Brigitte said. "Does the key have a number?"

"No," I said. I rubbed my fingers on the rough edges of the key.

"Well, while you're figuring it out, we need to feed . . . feed . . ." Brigitte looked at her clipboard for her next client. "Sylvie."

I guessed Sylvie was another dog. Brigitte put the petmobile in drive and crawled into traffic, her nose inches from the windshield. She drove so slowly that I realized that earlier she *had* been hurrying.

"And maybe *un petit morceau de gâteau*?" Henri asked.

What was it with boys and food? My brothers couldn't

go fifteen minutes without eating, and Henri had been hanging with us for an entire hour. He must've been starving. I had to admit, a little cake even sounded good to me right now.

"There is a shop in Sylvie's building," Brigitte said. "We feed her first."

She parked in front of another apartment building. This one was newer and more modern than the other building. It was very clean and stark white, from the first to the eighth floor, and lacked the decor, details, and golden embellishments of Fifi's building and la place Vendôme, which both seemed hundreds of years older.

I put the ribbon and key around my neck and continued thinking about what the key could open. Brigitte put Fifi in a little pink purse and handed it to Henri. "You can carry Fifi," she said. The doorman at this building also nodded like Brigitte was an important guest and we were too because we were with her. He held the door open for us.

When we got to the apartment, Brigitte said, "Wait here. The owners don't like it when people walk around here." She took a pair of plastic booties that looked like shower caps out of a lab coat pocket and slid one onto each shoe. With her big key chain she unlocked the door to a foyer that could've popped out of a magazine. Everything was white—walls, tile, furniture—and it smelled like Mom's Pine-Sol cleaner. She walked down the hall and into a room, where she spoke in French. "*Bonjour*, Sylvie. You are so pretty. Are you hungry? Here you go." She waited. "Do you think that's yummy? Yes, you do." She came out of the room with a giant snake wrapped around her shoulders like a pashmina.

I shrieked and jumped back.

"Whoa!" Henri yelled. "That is a snake!"

My eyes bulged. "Do you know it's around your neck? Could it strangle you?"

"Do not be silly. Sylvie is very gentle. And isn't she pretty? She likes it when you tell her she's pretty."

"Pretty snake," I said to Sylvie. *Please don't kill Brigitte, or me, or Henri*, I thought. Sylvie's neck stretched around something round, like an egg or tennis ball.

"What's that?" I asked. "A tumor?"

"This? No. Not a tumor. She just had lunch. A rat."

I held back the urge to gag. I hoped she hadn't taken that out of her pocket too. Were there more rats in the petmobile?

"Let's get her out for a while. I think she's lonely," Brigitte said. "She likes to be around people. We will take her with us for cake." She looked at the snake. "Do you like the sound of that? *Le gâteau?*" She lifted Sylvie's head for us to see. "She is smiling. She likes cake."

We were really going for cake with . . . *wait for it* . . . a six-foot snake.

"Fab," I said. "It'll wash down that mouse."

"Rat," Brigitte corrected me.

Brigitte slid the booties back off her feet and into her pocket, took an empty canvas bag from a hook, and locked the door, and the four of us went to the lobby, where there was a small *boulangerie*.

I anticipated a negative reaction to Sylvie followed by terrible embarrassment, so I was super glad when Brigitte curled her up and put her into the canvas bag and zipped it almost all the way shut. Through the opening she said to Sylvie, "You are very pretty."

11

All the desserts looked so good. I ordered a cream puff with chocolate sauce. Brigitte got a baguette, and Henri salivated over a slice of strawberry savarin. We sat, and Brigitte dropped pieces of bread into the canvas bag sitting in the chair next to her. "It's not as good as the rat, eh?" she asked through the hole in the bag.

I examined my phone. "Let's see where the other teams are." I opened Twister.com. "I don't know why I didn't think of this sooner," I said as the site opened. I scanned it. "Looks like no one has made it to the third clue yet. That's good. This is our chance to get in the lead." I took the key off my neck. "We've just gotta get there first, and I want another chance with Murielle duPluie. If we come in first, she'll have a good story about a team going from tenth to first place. Wouldn't that be great?" I finally took a bite of my puff. Henri's plate was empty.

I peeked into the canvas bag to see that the first several inches of Sylvie's body were in the shape of a baguette.

"May I see *la clé*?" Henri asked.

I took the key off my neck and gave it to him.

He studied it while I ate, not like my brothers, but as fast as I could in a ladylike way, because I didn't want my puff to end up in Henri's stomach or Sylvie's neck.

Brigitte took a place mat and turned it over. She pulled a pencil out of another lab coat pocket. That coat was amazing. It was like a Mary Poppins coat. "Let's play a game." She made blank dashes and a hangman symbol. "Pick a letter."

"Game? We don't have time. We need to concentrate on that key," I said.

"A quick game exercises the brain," Brigitte said. "It will think better when you are done."

"I love games," Henri said. "I pick *A*."

She wrote in *A*s where they belonged.

How could they be playing a game at a time like this?

It didn't last long. Henri guessed it was "Sylvie is a pretty snake."

He looked at the key again. "There are a lot of books at the hotel. Let's go there and look for ideas."

Since we didn't have any other leads, we decided to go back to the hotel.

"We will return Sylvie to her home first?" Henri asked Brigitte.

Brigitte asked Sylvie, who was still in the bag, "Do you want to go home, my sweetie?" She glanced at the snake's face. "No, she does not want to go home yet."

Fifi licked Henri again. "How about Fifi?" he asked.

"She is having so much fun. She will love the old hotel," Brigitte said as we got back into the petmobile and secured Fifi into her car seat.

Henri huffed like he wasn't happy to be driving around with a pooch and a snake. Maybe I could change the subject. "I love the old hotel too."

"It was a mansion for guests who could not fit in the king's castle at the holidays," Henri said. "When the city grew up, the hotel, it stay the same as before."

"I like that it feels old. Do you like working—oh no." I cut myself off when I saw who was waiting at the front of the hotel.

"Mon Dieu," Henri said at the sight of Jean-Luc, Sabine, and Robert.

"Oh, look," Brigitte said. "There are your friends." She honked the barking horn and waved to them like they were well acquainted. *"Bonjour!"* she called out the window.

Henri sank into the seat, but there really was no way to hide in the petmobile. "What are they doing here?"

I said, "Maybe they feel bad about what happened at la place de la Concorde and they want to apologize."

"Pfft," Henri said. I think the English translation of that would've been "no freakin' way."

We pulled into one of the hotel's four parking spots.

"Can you get Fifi?" Brigitte asked Henri. "Put her in her pink *sac*. She likes riding around in that." Her cell phone rang. "I will come in *un moment*." She answered it, *"Boutique Brigitte—Pour les Petits Animaux."*

Henri walked toward his three former friends with a white puffy pup in a pink bag over his shoulder. He stood up straight. *"Comment?"*—What?—he asked them, as tough as possible.

"Beau sac," Jean-Luc said.

"Pink is your color," Robert added.

"Stop it," Sabine said to them. "Pink is the new black." Then to Henri she said, "We came to see how you were doing with the key." Now she was trying to be nice? Something fishy was going on here. Fish? Would that be Brigitte's next pet?

"Really?" Henri asked.

"You know, six minds are better than three," she said.

"Like a partnership?" I asked.

"*Pfft,*" Henri said.

"Yeah, *pfft,*" I added. "We're way close to solving this clue. We're not gonna help you."

Brigitte, who finished with her call, joined us with Sylvie's bag, the snake's head now poking out through the hole for air.

Jean-Luc's, Sabine's, and Robert's eyes popped out at the sight.

"Afraid of a pretty little snake?" I asked them. "There's no way you'll be able to go to where this clue leads if you're afraid of stuff."

"*Comment?*" Henri asked me.

"Oh, don't worry," I said to him. "I won't give it away. Even if I did, they would be too afraid to follow through."

Just then the lacrosse bus pulled up. Perfect timing. We all stood and watched the muddy, tired American lacrosse team get off.

I could see Mom sitting in the last row of the bus. I took out my phone and sent her a quick text that, if things went the way I hoped, would help with this little thing I was doing to Henri's so-called friends.

JTC each offered me a high five on their way by.

"Victory," Josh said.

"Another win," Topher said.

"We advance to the next round," Charlie said.

They followed their team into the hotel.

Mom came up to us and glanced at her phone like I thought she would when she heard my message arrive. She said to me, "An abandoned metro station? I don't think so, Gwen," she said.

"Shh—Mom," I said, and bent my neck toward our three competitors, like she'd spilled some majorly secret and important beans in front of the opposing team.

"What? It's too dangerous. And sorry, but I'm too exhausted to go with you. We can talk about it tomorrow." Then she looked at Brigitte. "Pretty snake." She petted Fifi and departed.

Sabine, Jean-Luc, and Robert whispered to each other.

Jean-Luc said, "Since your mommy won't let you go to the old *metro* station at night, we will go on ahead and just beat you to another clue. Then we will tell the other teams where to go, and you will be last again."

They walked off, laughing. Robert barked.

"I do not know what . . . what was that?" Henri asked.

"I knew that was exactly what my mom would say, so I made up something to text her. And, presto, those three morons are off on a wild goose chase," I said.

"They are chasing a goose? Is that like a duck?" Henri asked.

"No. Sorry. It's just an expression. It means that they are off in the wrong direction, wasting their time."

"I am glad they are chasing ducks," Henri said. "You are . . ." He pointed to his head.

"Thanks," I said. "I have three older brothers who've taught me pretty much every trick in the book."

"What book?" Henri asked.

"Never mind. Sorry, there isn't a book."

"Yes, there is," Henri said. "Inside. Let's look for the key in the hotel books."

"Okay," I said.

"Do you want to go in the hotel?" Brigitte asked Sylvie, who was still nestled in the bag. "She does."

12

Brigitte and Henri went into the lobby, but I walked to the corner where Knit Cap was. He was singing, "It's time . . . my time . . . my time to fly . . ."

The words were familiar, but the tune wasn't.

Coincidence?

"Did you write those lyrics?" I asked.

"Yup. Ages ago. But I couldn't finish it. I'm good at the music, but not the lyrics."

"That's funny. I'm just the opposite. I write lots of lyrics, but not music," I said. "But those words you were just singing. Do you know they were part of the Shock Value contest?"

"Yeah. It's all over Twister."

That made sense.

Then he asked me, "If you write lyrics, then you must sing?"

"Um. No. Not so much," I said. "My brothers say that I sound like a dying hyena when I sing."

"You know," he said, "sometimes brothers say things that aren't true just to be mean." He strummed. "Give it a try: 'It's time to fly.'"

My brothers did a lot to be mean; that was true. I glanced around, and no one I knew was in earshot.

He coaxed me again. "It's time to fly," he sang.

I inhaled deeply and softly sang, "It's time—"

"Louder."

I inhaled again. "It's time to FLLLLYYYYYY!"

Knit Cap took his sunglasses off and looked at me with widened eyes. "O-M-G."

"That bad?" I asked. "I told you. Hyena."

"No. Your brothers stink. You're really good. Try again." He played the lead again and I sang.

People walking by threw money in the open guitar case. "If you hang with me, I'll be rich," he said.

"Unlikely," I said.

He craned his neck toward my royal blue bag. "The key?"

"Yeah. Any ideas what it might open?" I asked. "I want to get there first so that Murielle duPluie can do a story about us in first place!"

"I have a few ideas," he said. "It's a game, so there might not be an actual lock."

"Duh." Of course. "Lock is too obvious," I said. "But what else could a key lead to?"

"That, my new singing friend, is the question. You need to think deep. You're like a poet if you write lyrics. Musicians and poets think really deep. That's why you know what I'm saying." He strummed a chord. "Good luck."

"Thanks," I said, and walked toward the hotel door, even though I wasn't entirely convinced that he knew what he was talking about.

13

The old hotel lobby was cozy and dimly lit, but bustling with chaos tonight—infested with a sweaty lacrosse team and their parents. In a particularly dark corner Beef, Professor Camponi, and his nurse huddled around the key like it was a crystal ball and they were waiting for it to reveal its secrets.

Professor Camponi scratched his chin and looked off in the distance, thinking deeply.

Henri watched them too. "Do you think we can check the book of tricks and send them to get the ducks?"

I grinned.

"I think we can come up with something," I said. My mind searched through all kinds of tricks my brothers had played on me. Like the time JTC sent me an invitation to MaryEllen Marini's costume party, which might have been okay if I was actually invited to her party and it had been a costume party.

"You work here," I said, still thinking through the details. "That'll be a big help with this."

"Is that what the trick book says?" he asked.

At some point I'd have to tell him again there wasn't an actual book of tricks. But now that I thought about it, maybe there should be. "Do you have any royal blue paper?"

"I think I can find some," he said.

I waited for him as he fetched the paper.

Brigitte looked at her watch. "I need to bring Fifi and Sylvie home. I will leave you two in charge of the ducks, okay?"

We agreed.

Brigitte said, "I will pick you up in the morning after I go to the Cliquots. I have an important pet delivery to make for them."

"That sounds good. My mom won't let me out anymore tonight anyway," I said. "Brigitte, thanks for taking me on this hunt. I know you have your job to do, but I wouldn't be able to do it without you."

"That is what big sisters are for," she said. Then to Sylvie and Fifi she said in French, "Come on, precious babies, I'll put you to bed." She called as she left, *"Bonne soirée!"* A few seconds later I heard the bark of a horn as she drove away.

"I have it," Henri said about the paper.

"Is there a place where we can work?" I asked.

"I know a place. It is perfect." Henri walked into a corner of the lobby and slipped behind a tree in a flowerpot. The wall was lined with dark woodwork and busy with elaborate oil paintings of royalty. He pushed in a piece of wood molding. That triggered a slim section of the wall to shift aside, providing a narrow entrance. Henri squeezed through it. After a quick glance behind me, when I saw the lacrosse team and parents all chatting and distracted, I did the same. It was totally Scooby Doo.

The wooden door slid closed after me, and we were in pitch black. "I can't see."

"Un moment." Henri turned on a flashlight app on his phone and led the way through a narrow passageway.

"What is this?"

"Halls behind the walls. They lead to . . . you know . . . tubes under Paris."

"Tunnels?"

"*Oui*. Tunnels."

"What for?"

"During wars, people needed to hide and move around in secret," he said. "But today it is just halls." He stopped at a section where we could hear people talking on the other side.

"Listen," I said. It was Beef.

Henri moved a playing card–size piece of wood affixed to the inside of the wall. It revealed several holes, each a bit bigger than a pin. He turned off his flashlight and squinted to look through a hole, and I did the same. We spied into the lobby.

Beef spoke to Professor Camponi. "I've got to get those backstage tickets. Don't you understand?"

The nurse answered, "You must really love Shock Value."

"Who doesn't love Shock Value? But, it's more than that. So, so much more," she said, without offering the deets. "I just need the good professor here to solve the clues to make sure I win. Capeesh?" Professor Camponi nodded. "Good. Because if you don't, it's bye-bye to the free tours, and you won't be able to give your grand-daughter the tickets she's wanted since the last concert."

"When was that?" the nurse asked.

"The one our friend Clay Bright didn't make it to," Beef said. "Camponi's only granddaughter was going to that concert, which was obviously canceled when Clay decided to go all Houdini and disappear. She never got to see her favorite band. Now Grandpa has a chance to be her hero. I'll get a backstage pass and he can get the tickets," Beef said. She turned to look at Professor Camponi directly. "You got that, Camponi?"

Professor Camponi nodded and gave a thumbs-up.

14

Henri slid the wooden card back in front of the holes and turned the flashlight on again. I was about to talk about what Beef had said when Henri put his hand over my mouth and whispered, "Shh." He walked further down the secret corridor and into a small, dark room. With matches from his back pocket he lit candle sconces hanging on the wall. It was an old office with worn and cracked leather chairs. Dust and cobwebs covered every surface.

Who would need an office hidden behind the hotel walls?

Henri took his sleeve, pulled it down over his hand, and used it to wipe off a large section of the desk, where he set the royal blue paper and black pen.

"This is a great hidden room," I said.

"I love that it is like . . ." He made an "oooooo" sound, like a ghost.

"You mean scary."

"Yeah. You think?"

"With three older brothers I've been scared by the best of them. It takes a lot to freak me out."

He nodded, but I didn't know if he understood "freak out." "What are you going to write?" he asked.

"I'm gonna write a letter to myself." I wrote, *To Gwen Russell.* "It will be from a Shock Value representative. It'll have information about the key. When Beef sees a royal blue message for me, and she hasn't gotten one, she won't be able to resist reading it."

"And she will go look for the duck that you write about in the note?"

"Exactly."

"I am glad you have older brothers," he said.

I wrote the rest of the note in my most grown-up handwriting. It said:

Most people from Paris know there is a basement in Orly airport with lockers where employees store their belongings. Since you are American, we thought it was fair for us to tell you because you would have no way of knowing this.

Good luck.

From,

The Shock Value Team

Henri asked, "She will go to Orly looking for a basement that is not there?"

"Right. Plus, she'll think that they're somehow giving me extra help because I'm American, and that will make her mad. If she's mad, maybe she'll make a mistake."

I folded the note and gave it to Henri. "Can you put this out on the front desk tomorrow morning? Place it where you're sure she'll see it."

"*Oui.*"

Henri blew out the two candles and led me through the secret corridors back into the lobby, which was now empty. My phone vibrated. I looked at the text. It was from Josh. He said Mom was looking for me. I said, "I have to go."

"*Bonne soirée*, Gwen," Henri said.

"*Bonne soirée*, Henri," I said. "Thanks for your help."

"You can wait and thank me when we are in the front row!"

I ran up the center staircase, taking the steps two at a time. I slowed and turned my head to look back, and at the exact moment, Henri turned his head and our eyes met.

15

When I came down in the morning, my mom and JTC were ready to leave for the next round of lacrosse games.

"Behave for Brigitte," she said to me, and she gave me money for lunch. "And wish your brothers luck."

"*Bonne chance,*" I called to JTC. They shoved several mini breakfast tarts into their mouths, stuffing their cheeks like chipmunks, and gave me the peace sign.

One quick look at the front desk and I immediately saw the royal blue paper. I made myself a plate of grapes and tarts, pretending I had no idea it was there.

Beef entered the hotel through its huge wooden door, which was complete with tarnished golden handle and hinges.

I concentrated on my grapes and looked out the window for the arrival of the petmobile. I wondered if Fifi and Sylvie would be with us today. As embarrassing as that van was to drive around in, I'd grown strangely attached to it and its passengers. After a while you got used to its unique appearance and odor.

Beef was instantly attracted to the blue paper. Without hesitation she walked toward it and spoke to the concierge. "Hiya, Étienne, how're you doing this fine morning?"

I backed up behind the tree in the flowerpot.

"*Bonjour*, Madame LeBoeuf. It is a beautiful day."

"I see you have this note for one of the members of my next tour. I'd be happy to deliver it for you."

"I thought your tours were canceled today, Madame."

"You are on the ball, Étienne. They were. But I will see this girl this morning. And I'd be happy to deliver this for you."

"*Oui, merci*, Madame LeBoeuf. That would be kind of you."

"Don't mention it. Unless I ever need a favor, in which case I'll mention it. Ha-ha!" She took the note with a big smile. "I'm just joshing you, Étienne."

"Oh. Ha-ha. Joshing. I understand." He smiled broadly.

I saw her slide the royal blue note into her pocket, scan the lobby, and leave.

From my view through the tree leaves, I saw Knit Cap sitting cross-legged in an armchair, studying the people and activity while sipping coffee that was for hotel guests. It seemed like he made himself right at home in the lobby, which was strange because he wasn't a guest. He'd watched what Beef had just done. Then he found me between the greens and raised his cup in a gesture that suggested he knew the trick I'd just played. Of course he didn't have his sunglasses on inside, and without them there was something familiar about his face.

I came out of my hiding place.

"That had something to do with the key?" he asked.

"Yeah," I said.

"Good for you," he said. "Now you're playing the game. And remember that games and puzzles are more challenging if they provide misdirection." He stood and swung his guitar over his shoulder and went on his way.

Then I saw the petmobile drive up the boulevard.

Did I say I was becoming attached to the petmobile? The basketball nose was now a beak, and large foam feathers had been stuck to the sides. The horn announced Brigitte's arrival with a *Squaaawk!*

I ran out front to see what this transformation of the petmobile meant. Tourists photographed the wheeled bird, but the locals didn't seem to notice or care.

Brigitte took a while to find the perfect parking spot, just like she seemed to do everywhere in Paris. *"Bonjour!"* she called to me. She had on a green lab coat today, which was equally as dirty as yesterday's black one. This one was speckled with white and black droplets that I suspected were bird poop. On her head she wore a hat with a long beak.

"Good morning," I said. "How about we talk in the van?" I thought that would get us away from the onlookers—including Knit Cap, now strumming—who had gathered.

"I would love some tea," Brigitte said, and walked toward the lobby.

She said hello to Étienne and briefly discussed the bashful personality of his pet turtle. Then he made her a cup of tea and placed a scone from the complimentary breakfast bar on a china plate. She and I sat on a sofa in the lobby. It seemed that everywhere we went, Brigitte was treated like royalty. It's true: people like people who care for their pets.

Henri joined us with a plate stacked a foot high with scones, muffins, and mini bagels. He was such a boy!

"The book of tricks worked," he said.

"What book of tricks?" Brigitte asked.

We filled her in on what we'd done while trying to spy on Beef, who sat in a leather armchair with her feet propped on an ottoman, toggling between her watch and her smartphone.

"I bet she's looking up stuff about the airport," I said.

"No, thank you. I do not like bets," Henri said. "Usually someone loses." I really needed to watch my expressions around him.

Beef put her phone down and whipped a pocket-knife out of her fanny pack. She twisted a toothpick out of it and went at her teeth—poking and picking.

I touched the key around my neck and felt each groove and bend. When my fingers felt a small nub at the end, through which the ribbon was looped, I took it off. I rubbed the nub and, squeezing a little, turned it. It twisted like a cap on a tube of toothpaste.

It opened.

"Look," I quietly said to Brigitte and Henri, but they were already watching. I turned the key upside down, and a tiny piece of rolled paper slid out. I screwed the top back on and unrolled the paper.

"It says: '*I leap off* is written here.'"

I looked at Henri and Brigitte for a reaction but got

none. Brigitte shook her head like *I don't know,* and Henri shrugged his shoulders.

Henri said, *"La bibliothèque?"* The library? "Everything is written there."

"I guess it could be. Or a plaque somewhere?" I suggested.

Neither of them had any idea. I keyed the phrase into the search engine on my phone. Nothing.

"I guess we should go to the library," I said.

"That is good," Brigitte said. "I can drop the Cliquots' pets off at the groomer on the way."

"I thought you were a groomer too." We headed out to a beautifully sunny Paris day.

Henri lagged behind.

"Not for this kind of pet," Brigitte said. Based on the feathers and beak I had a feeling I was going to find some kind of bird in the mobile.

I got into the front seat and turned to look behind me, and I did in fact find a bird. Correction: birds. Blue and orange parrots. Three cages full.

Brigitte hopped into the front seat, buckled up, and checked the rearview, each side mirror, and the rearview again. When Henri came to the mobile, his pockets were stuffed with something. I knew what it was because I had brothers. Food.

He climbed into the backseat and Brigitte asked, "Ready to go?"

Then every bird, all twelve of them, repeated, "Ready to go?" "Ready?" "Go?" "Ready to go?" They weren't in unison.

Henri jumped back in shock. "They *talk*?"

"The best kind of feathered friend," Brigitte said.

"Fantastique," Henri muttered, but I sensed he meant *un-fantastique.*

When Brigitte backed out of the parking spot, the petmobile made a *Beep! Beep! Beep!*

A dozen parrots mimicked, "Beep! Beep! Beep!"

Henri, who was closer to the flock, covered his ears. On his hands' way to his ears, he popped a mini muffin into his mouth.

"Here we go," Brigitte said.

"Here we go!" "Here we go!" "Here!" "Go!"

16

Brigitte pulled into a lovely cobblestone alley with creeping ivy and flowers. She honked the *Squaaawk!* horn to scoot a few stray cats out of her way. She opened the mobile's back door and carried one cage of four birds through a small door next to a faded sign covered almost entirely by vines. The sign said BAIN D'OISEAU.

"Bird bath," Henri translated for me.

"Bath?" "BATH?" "Baaaath?" "BAAAATTH?"

The remaining parrots did not like the idea. Brigitte

came back, and when she heard them yelling, she asked, "You told them?"

"Not exactly. They kind of overheard us talking. You might want to explain to them that eavesdropping is rude," I said as she carried in the second cage, which contained four nervous birds yelling about a bath.

"They are freaking out," Henri said, using one of my expressions.

I agreed, "Yes, they are."

"They're freaking out!" "Freaking!" "OUT!" they said. One shouted, "Baath?" and the remaining three started flipping out about the bath all over again.

Once Brigitte brought the last cage inside, the pet-mobile was filled with beautiful quiet, and I was able to think about "I leap off." But the quiet didn't help. I still had no ideas where that might be written.

Brigitte drove to the library via a road that ran parallel to the Seine, the main river flowing through the center of Paris. I watched a tour boat glide down the water.

"I really want to take one of those river tours," I said.

"Want me to stop at the ticket station?" Brigitte asked.

"No thanks. Winning this contest is more important."

We arrived at the library. "Wait," I said when I saw Jean-Luc, Sabine, and Robert parking.

"Do you think they found 'I leap off'?" Brigitte asked.

"Let's watch them for a second," I said. "Stay still and they won't even know we're here."

"I'll just back into this spot behind the bushes," Brigitte said. She put the petmobile in reverse and *Beep! Beep! Beep!*

Jean-Luc, Robert, and Sabine looked over and had a good hearty laugh at the van's new ensemble. They cupped their hands by their noses like beaks and hooted.

"Owls hoot," Brigitte explained to us. "Not parrots. They are so stupid."

"Let's just get in there and find the book where 'I leap off' is written before they do," I said.

On my way out, my foot stepped on a paper on the petmobile floor. It was the place mat that Brigitte and Henri had played hangman on.

It's a game.

Puzzle.

Misdirection.

"Hang on," I said. "I don't think 'I leap off' is written in a book. Well, maybe It is, but that's not the clue."

Brigitte said, "But it says—"

"We've been thinking about this wrong. Each clue needs to be solved, like a puzzle." I wrote, *I leap off is written here* on a blank section of the place mat. "Do you know what anagrams are?"

"Letters that are like . . ." Henri pantomimed stirring something in a bowl.

"Mixed up," I said. "Letters have to be rearranged. Maybe if we rearrange these, they will reveal the real clue."

I played with the letters:

At top.

Irish.

Brigitte added:

Pet Fifi.

White leaf.

"That's the idea," I said. "We just have to make them into a location."

"I can," Henri said as though it took no effort at all.

"You can. *What?*"

"You cannot see it?" he asked.

I looked at the letters. "No! What is it?"

"I will give you hints and you figure it out," he said.

Jean-Luc, Sabine, and Robert ran out of the library and to their car.

"No!" I yelled, louder than I meant. "Maybe they've figured it out. We are in a huge hurry! Just tell us what it is."

He looked disappointed with my anger.

"I'm sorry," I said. "I just really want these tickets."

"D'accord," he said. "It's the Eiffel Tower. You have a few letters left over, but it's pretty close."

"Very close. Too close to be wrong. Let's go!"

Brigitte skipped the triple mirror check and recheck and pulled out with a lot more power this time. The power of a sloth!

"First place, here we come!" I called.

17

Brigitte passed one side of the Eiffel Tower. We couldn't park on that street, so she made several turns until we came up on the other side. Under one of the iron lattice archways a girl in a royal blue shirt—different from the last one—was waiting, stretching her gum out of her mouth with one hand and scrolling on her phone with the other.

Brigitte couldn't park here either, so Henri and I jumped out and sprinted toward the girl.

When Blue Shirt looked up from her phone, we were in her face.

"Whoa," she said, startled. "Where did you come from?"

"We ran," I gasped.

She reached into a box and took out a royal blue gift bag. I peeked into the box. There were nine others.

We were first!

"Where is Murielle duPluie?" This was my chance to redeem myself to the world. After all, I was representing the USA! "Does she want to interview us?"

"Nope. She's chasing another story today."

"Maybe we could give you a statement or something to send to the TV news," I suggested. I really wanted public attention for this achievement.

"Nah. That's okay." She went back to her phone. "Good luck," she added without looking up.

"What is the clue?" Henri asked, but I was still thinking about my missed moment in the spotlight. If Murielle duPluie wasn't going to report on us, then I had to take matters into my own hands. *Isn't that what social media is for?*

I logged onto Twister.com and typed in a post: *Hello! Can't tell you where we are or where we're headed, but this team is . . . wait for it . . . in first place!*

That was a good start, but I still wanted the shout-out on TV!

"Come here. Hold up the bag—we're gonna do a sel-fie." I snapped a pic of me, Henri, and the bag without getting the Eiffel Tower in the background. The longer we could maintain a lead, the better.

Back in the petmobile we opened the bag.

I keep the torch lit for all to see,

The apple of their eye,

Tall and strong for liberty,

I watch the birds and planes fly by.

48-51-0/2-16-47

A surge of excitement flowed through my veins. "OMG! I know this! I know the answer to this clue!"

"So fast?" Henri asked.

"Yes. It's the Statue of Liberty! She has a torch and she's the symbol of liberty. And the part about the apple—that's what we call New York City, the Big Apple, and that's where she is. She stands on an island where she can watch birds and planes fly by."

"That sounds like the right answer, but we cannot go to New York for the next clue," Brigitte said.

"True," I agreed. "Do you have something like a Statue of Liberty here?"

Henri laughed. "Actually, we have three."

98

18

"There are *three* Statues of Liberty in Paris?" I asked. Wow, the one in New York Harbor had suddenly become less special. "At least we're in the lead, so we'll have time to go to all of them."

"We don't have to," Brigitte said.

"We do!" I agreed. "We have to be first. We're gonna beat Beef."

"I mean we only have to go to one of the statues," Brigitte said. "The correct one."

"How will I know which one is correct?" I asked.

Brigitte pointed to the numbers. "I use these kinds of numbers all the time to find my customers' homes."

"Like a cell phone number?" I asked.

"No. They are coordinates for a GPS," she said. "They are the exact location of the next clue."

"Well, what are we waiting for? *Allons-y!*" I said. "Let's go!"

Brigitte took a gadget out of the glove box and punched in the numbers from the clue. Instantly, a voice told us in French to turn right. Brigitte, hands clenched on the ten o'clock and two o'clock positions on the wheel, did as the voice said.

We were only a few blocks away from our destination when an alarm sounded from Brigitte's watch. She pushed a little button to make it stop. She swung the petmobile into a U-turn.

"What are you doing?" I asked.

"It is time to pick up the birds from their baths."

"But the statue?" I whined.

"Work first," she sang as if I would totally understand.

Fine, I understood, but there was a lot at stake here besides a few wet birds.

She maneuvered through the steep winding streets of Montmartre, past street-side painters and people sitting outdoors sipping cappuccino.

Each of the three of us grabbed a birdcage from the *bain d'oiseau* and put the flock in the back of the minivan. The birds smelled good, like soap and flowers. "Here we go, guys," Brigitte called back to them. "To the Île aux Cygnes to get the next clue."

"Clue!" *"Cygnes."* "Guys." "Go!" The gang sounded less energetic than they had on the way to their bath this morning.

"Usually they nap after their—" She whispered "bath" very softly, so they wouldn't hear the word. "If you're quiet, they'll probably fall asleep."

We were ready to go, but Henri was nowhere to be found. I looked around the busy street until I saw the back of his head. He was at a small table-like wagon on the side of the road, paying a man. I joined him to see the table layered with rows of croissants. Henri held a bag open for me. "Croissant?"

While I was a stranger to the croissant, I had never met a pastry that I didn't like. So I took one and bit into it, and was pleasantly surprised by a warm, sweet glob of chocolate hiding inside the flaky, buttery roll.

"It is good, *non?*" Henri asked.

"Non. I mean, *oui.* It's very good."

Back in the petmobile the three of us rode in croissant-induced silence. Other cars whizzed around us. We passed the Eiffel Tower and drove onto a bridge that crossed the Seine. Brigitte pointed off the side of the bridge to a small protrusion of land, but I was already looking at it. It was an exact replica of our Statue of Liberty. I couldn't believe my eyes. It was like her twin, her smaller twin.

"Pull over," I said. "I think we're first!"

"First!" "First!" "First!"

"Shhh," Brigitte said. "You woke them up. They get cranky if they don't get a nap. And you would not like them when they are grouchy."

"Sorry. But this is a race! Can you just pull over and let me out?"

"I cannot stop here," Brigitte said. "I will park ahead. We will have to walk." She eased into a parking space, painfully slowly.

"Or run," Henri said. "Race you!" He took off toward the statue.

I chased him. This time I ran as fast as I could, but I couldn't catch up. I wasn't trying to be girly; I seriously couldn't keep up. Was I getting slower? It was one thing to pretend to be slow; it was another to actually become slow.

Henri stopped at the Shock Value rep. It was the same girl from the Louvre.

"*Bonjour,*" Henri said.

"Hi," I gasped. "Are we first?"

"Yes, you are. You really are a comeback story," she said.

"Where is Murielle duPluie?"

"On another story," she said. "Here is the last clue. Don't get too comfy with first place; this one is really hard."

"Jeez, can't Murielle duPluie send someone else?" I groaned. "This is major music news."

Brigitte caught up with us. Totally out of breath, she asked, "What does the clue say?"

I read:

"*XX marks the spot. Number eighty-three is the place. In the Garden of Names.*"

I looked at them. "Do you guys have any ideas?"

They both shook their heads.

I looked off in the distance. I could see the Eiffel Tower, and dark clouds starting to roll in. They looked nasty.

Brigitte saw them too. "Let's get the birds home," she said.

We hustled to the petmobile, where our feathered friends were still snoozing. We closed the doors as quietly as we could.

I read the clue out loud again. "'*XX* marks the spot.

Number eighty-three is the place. In the Garden of Names.'" Still no one had any ideas.

One of the birds said, "Eighty-three! In the garden!" in its sleep.

Another answered, "Okay, Sammy," in its sleep. "Deliver the flowers."

"They talk in their sleep?"

"Yeah. They say some funny things sometimes. Stuff they've overheard. Their owner is a florist. So they say stuff they hear from the store or the cart."

"What cart?"

"The owner has a flower cart. The birds who are well behaved get to hang out on it on nice days. They love it," she said.

The rest of the afternoon we spent my lunch money on crepes smothered in Nutella and took the birds around the city. As the afternoon turned into evening, we planned to take the tired flock home.

Brigitte drove at her usual glacial speed that I was starting to get used to when rain started hitting the windshield hard.

"Oh no," said Brigitte.

"What is the matter?" Henri asked.

"I do not like driving in the rain." Brigitte's hands trembled on the wheel.

Henri said, "It is okay. Take your time. We can stop at the hotel if you turn up there."

Just then a car flew past us and splashed water onto the windshield. Little tears formed in the corners of Brigitte's eyes.

"Almost there," I said to reassure her. I could see the hotel up ahead.

She coasted into her preferred parking space and turned off the ignition. "I cannot drive anymore in this weather. I will have to call the Cliquots to come and pick up the birds and they will probably fire me."

"You can bring the birds inside and wait for the rain to let up," I said.

"I do not think birds are allowed in the hotel," Henri said.

"What if no one knows they are there?" I asked.

"I have heard them. They are very . . ." Henri made a beak with his hand and mimicked the birds. "Go! Guys! Clue!" Just as he started yelling "Baaa—" I put my hand over his beak.

"But there is a room where they can stay," I suggested. "A very quiet room where no guests will see them. Can't we go there?"

"We will have to"—he tucked his head into his neck and made a swaying motion from side to side, then hid his face behind his hands—"around so that no one will see the birds in the lobby."

"Like, sneak?" I asked.

He nodded.

"Piece of cake," I said.

"*Le gâteau?* Where? Where is the cake?"

"I meant it will be easy to sneak them in."

"Really?" Brigitte asked. "There are twelve of them."

"But there are thirty lacrosse players coming in soon. They are waaay louder than some birds. Trust me," I said. "Call the Cliquots and tell them you don't want to drive the birds in the rain and you will keep them for the night and bring them home safe and sound in the morning. They won't fire you. They'll probably be glad that you are so safety conscious."

"Okay," she agreed.

I looked at my watch. We had about a half hour until the boys would be back. "Henri, I think the lobby could use some vacuuming. Let's go do that."

"Vacuuming?"

I made a motion like I was vacuuming, but maybe it looked more like I was mowing the lawn, because he didn't understand. I said, "Vrooooom," as though I was sucking up dirt. He looked like he still didn't understand.

"You know when the floor is dirty and you use a machine to suck up the dust?"

"What does the machine sound like?" he asked.

I said, "Vrooooomm." And I made a face like sucking up dirt.

He smiled. "Vroom. I like that. I never saw someone act like a vacuum before."

"You know the word 'vacuum'? Why didn't you say so?"

"Because it was more fun to watch you vrooom." He mimicked my face.

I punched him.

Darn.

Too hard again.

I really had to work on that.

"Sorry," I said when he rubbed his arm.

"*Pas de problème,*" he said. No problem.

19

Henri put on his hotel shirt and name tag. I wore a lab coat. If anyone asked, we would say that I worked for a cleaning company. Who knew that a few lab coats would come in so handy? I also donned some rubber gloves that Brigitte had in the back of the van.

"What are we going to do?" he asked.

"Move these chairs and plants to make a barrier that will be difficult for people to see behind. It will look like we are moving all of these things to vacuum behind and under them. Then we'll bring the birds in the front door, behind our barrier, and through the secret door," I said. "But in case someone happens to see through our barrier, it would be good to cover their cages." I looked up at the heavy drapes. "Do you think we can get one of these down for a little while?"

"Yes. I take them down to clean them. I can do it."

"Great," I said. "Once we move this stuff, we just need to wait for the team to arrive. When they come into the lobby, everything will be chaotic and loud. That's the perfect time to move the birds in."

He took down one of the drapes, which wasn't nearly as heavy as it had looked hanging up. I delivered it to the petmobile while he started sliding the chairs and potted plants. The rain was still coming down hard, so I ran. I jumped into the van and brought Brigitte up to speed.

"I spoke to the Cliquots," she said. "They were glad that I wasn't driving in the rain with their babies. They also said to make sure they get a good night's sleep."

"We can do that," I said.

"After we get them settled, they will look for dinner. I have food."

"When we move them in, can you cover them with this?" I handed her the fabric and she agreed.

On my sprint back to the hotel, I saw Knit Cap playing his guitar under an awning. I stopped to listen. He was singing a song about running away again—seemed like his theme—but then he paused at the same point that he did the other day. "Why do you stop when you get to that part?"

"I don't know how the rest goes," he said. "I don't have any more words."

"Words are my specialty," I said. "How about:

"I could go to Japan,
I could go to the sky,
If only I could fly."

"Wow. You're really good at this stuff." He strummed and added my words into his tune and then repeated "If only I could fly" several times as the refrain. It totally worked.

"That's good," I said.

"Good? It's better than good," he said. "Will you sing it with me?"

"Really?" I asked. I totally wanted to sing with him.

"Sure. A continuation of what we started yesterday." He played a chord and another and started it for me: "I could go to—"

I picked up: "Japan. I could go to the sky . . ."

He harmonized with me. We sounded great together. Really great!

When we finished the few lines, he said, "You have an amazing voice."

"Thanks." I think I blushed. Then I offered, "You can have those lyrics if you want."

"Thanks. That's a nice offer, but I want to write my own material," he said. "But tell me, how did you come up with that?"

"I like to start with a rhyme. This time with 'fly' and 'sky.' I make those two sentences and then fill in the others," I said. "But I keep a notebook and jot things down when they come to me. That would probably help you a lot."

I reached into my pocket where I'd stashed the few extra pieces of royal blue paper in case I needed them today. "This will help you start," I said. "It's easier to write lyrics than to try to just think them up."

"Wow. I'm gonna do that," he said. "Cool beans." He strummed and sang, "Cooool beansss."

"How long have you been playing?"

"All my life," he said.

"You're so good. Why do you play out here on the street when you could be at a club or something?"

"Been there, done that. As soon as I started playing for money, it wasn't about the music anymore; it was about the show and the publicity. I just love the music," he said.

"Me too," I agreed.

Then he said, "By the way, great job with the diversionary tactic you played on the Beefy lady. Too sly."

"Funny. I call her Beef too," I said. "I would've loved to have seen her face when she realized there were no basement lockers at the airport."

"I saw her mug when she got back here this morning," he said. "Wow, she was fuming. I think maybe she's onto you."

"She is?" Oh no, I never thought of what would happen if she figured out it was me. Beef didn't seem like a good person to have on your bad side. "I think I'll avoid her until this contest is over."

"And maybe even after that, like, forever," he suggested. "She is still furious about that TV reality show, and that was years ago."

"What happened?"

"She was a contestant on a super-popular talent discovery show. She lost, obviously, and never got over it."

"Is she a good singer?"

"Really good, actually. Country music," he said. "She still hopes to make it big, and I hope she does. Everyone deserves their big break."

Henri came outside and called to me, "I need help, Gwen."

"I have to go," I said to Knit Cap. "We're kind of doing something in there."

"Have fun, Gwen," he said. "I hope you win."

Henri had the lobby arranged perfectly. He asked, "Were you talking to the guitar player?"

"Yeah. His music is good," I said. "And he's nice."

"He is there all the time. I do not understand why someone who plays so well just stands on the street," Henri said.

"Because he loves the music. When he played for money, he said, it wasn't about the music anymore." Henri started pushing a vacuum along the edge of the newly exposed wall. "What are you doing?"

"Cleaning," he said with a grumpy tone. "Étienne asked me what I was doing. I told him. He got me the vacuum machine. So now I vacuum."

I smiled. The floor was kind of dirty behind all of this stuff.

Suddenly headlights flashed in the hotel window where the drapery was missing. "I think the team is back," I said.

The boys unloaded the bus from the front and back at the same time, shouting, "Vic-to-ry! Vic-to-ry!"

I signaled Brigitte and she took the first cage out of

the van, covered it with the fabric, and brought it to the door. As the boys entered the hotel, she handed the cage to me and I dashed along the pathway with it. No one even noticed me. I could hear the birds under the drape saying, "Vic-to-ry!"

I set the birds down in the secret hall and went back with the drape.

Brigitte brought in the next cage and we did the same thing.

When she came to the door with the third cage, the boys had a whole lacrosse game going on in the middle of the lobby. Étienne was telling them they couldn't play inside. They argued that it was raining outside and champions had to play.

We scooted the third cage in without issue.

Once the birds were all secured behind the wall, the three of us moved the furniture and plants back to their original places, which were now clean. I helped Henri rehang the drape and watched Knit Cap through the window as he jammed and jotted notes. He was way too good to be playing on the street.

JTC paused in their indoor game long enough to ask, "What are you doing, Gwen?"

"Oh, hey. Just helping straighten things up down

here. Like a little volunteering. No biggie. Congratulations on your win. That's exciting!"

"It's more than exciting!" Josh and Topher ran toward each other and crashed into a chest bump. "*It rocks!*" They high-fived after the body check.

Charlie asked, "How's the hunt for the tickets going?"

"It's going pretty well—"

Topher said, "Only you would waste your time in Paris playing some contest that you're never gonna win when you could be sightseeing."

Josh added, "Most girls would kill to shop in Paris."

"She's not a regular girl," Topher said. "She doesn't like shopping." The two of them moved away with their lacrosse sticks and tossed a ball back and forth. Étienne tried to get the ball, and they had a laugh playing monkey in the middle with him until the coach took the ball and all the sticks and made the team sit "like gentlemen" for dinner.

Before Charlie joined them, he said, "I think you're a regular girl. A guy would look funny in those capris and sandals." That was the closest thing to a compliment I could ever expect from JT or C.

Before he disappeared into the dining room, Josh called to me, "Hey, tell Shock Value I said hi. Especially Winston."

"I like Alec," Topher added.

"Dream big," Charlie said.

I sighed. "Sorry you had to see that," I said to Henri. "They can be such jerks sometimes, maybe most of the time, but sometimes they're nice. I just can't always tell which way it's gonna go. Usually when they're together like this with friends, it goes jerky."

"I understand," he said. "I have Jean-Luc, Robert, and Sabine. When they are together, they are . . . how you say? . . . jerky." I smiled. It was nice to have someone who kind of understood. I guess it didn't matter whether it was Paris or Pennsylvania—there were some things, like "jerky" groups, that were universal.

2 0

We uncovered the birdcages, fed the birds, and let them check out their temporary bedroom.

Henri lit the sconce candles before going on a search for pillows and blankets.

I texted Mom that Brigitte got a room in the hotel because of the bad weather and I was staying with her.

I heard Henri's voice in the lobby on the other side of the wall, so I slid the playing card–size wood chip aside and peeked in.

"Where have you been?" Étienne asked in French.

"I am doing the treasure hunt for the Shock Value tickets," Henri said in French, but I understood. I hadn't realized how much better my French had gotten in just a few days.

"Why are you doing that? You are probably the only person I know who doesn't like Shock Value," Étienne asked, again in French.

Henri shrugged.

Étienne said, "It is the girl, isn't it? The American. You like her?"

"We are having fun playing the game. She is not like other French girls I know. She likes sports."

"And you think she is pretty?"

"*Oui. Elle est jolie.*" Henri smiled.

I knew *jolie* meant "pretty." Henri thought I was pretty? And he was playing this whole game, missing work, and running all over Paris in a petmobile with a fluffy dog in a pink bag over his shoulder looking for tickets to see a band that he didn't even like? For me?

The birds were awake now, but calm and full-bellied.

"They talk less when they are calm," Brigitte said. "This is a good room for them, because there isn't a lot for them to see or hear."

I stopped listening through the wall when Henri came in with sleeping stuff. It seemed like the birds were still listening, but they weren't talking. I figured as long as no one mentioned that they were taking a bath, they would be quiet.

Henri returned stocked with everything we needed to camp out in the old office, including a board game and a white box wrapped in a pink satin ribbon. "Here." He handed it to me.

A gift?

I pulled the silk ribbon, easily untying it. Lifting the lid, I discovered rows of delicate little cookie-like sandwiches. Each one had three layers—the outer two pieces were the same color, and the middle layer was different.

"What are these?" I asked

"Have you never seen a *macaron*?"

"Yeah. I've seen them made with a lot of coconut and dipped in chocolate."

"Ah, that is not a French *macaron*." He pointed to one that had two dark brown layers sandwiching a whitish one. "That is espresso and cream." He pointed to another, which had a dark brown layer between two red pieces. "That's chocolate and raspberry." And he went on to name each *macaron* in the box, lying next to one another, creating a rainbow of colors: peanut butter and marshmallow, white chocolate and peppermint, pistachio and almond, etc. . . .

I took the cherry and vanilla one—it was about the

size of an Oreo—and bit it. It was crunchy and airy at the same time. "Mmmm. It's good. I want to try them all."

"Of course," Henri said. "They're little." He took the other half of the one I'd just bitten. I bit into another, and again he took the other half, until I'd eaten half of a dozen flavors!

"It's official. I like French *macarons*," I announced.

Henri smiled. "Me too."

Then we spread the blankets and put the pillows in a circle with enough room for a board game. Henri tossed me the dice to go first.

I heard voices in the lobby, but since they weren't bothering the birds, I ignored them and rolled. Double sixes! I was off to a good start.

Brigitte took her turn; then it was Henri's.

"Wait," I said. "Listen."

"It's just guests," Henri said.

"Not just any guests. I know that voice," I said. "That's Beef." I got up from my pile of blankets and walked over to the wood that blocked the pinholes. I slid it aside to see Beef talking to Professor Camponi.

It was the middle of the conversation. "You really let me down today. We're not gonna get those tickets." I wasn't positive, but I thought Beef might've wiped a tear. "I can't believe I let that girl outsmart me."

21

The next morning, the birds were fluttering around in their cages.

"They're hungry," Brigitte said through a yawn. "I'll feed them and get them back home on my route today. I also need to pick up today's client."

I didn't want to know what she would come back with. Kangaroo? Hippo?

She put food in their cages.

"We need to finish this hunt in first place. Then Murielle duPluie will report on us and I won't be an embarrassment to my country," I said. "This clue could be our big break."

"Big break!" "Win contest!" "Meet Shock Value!" "Get my big break!" "Sing for them!"

"What did they say?" Henri said.

"Something about singing for Shock Value and getting their big break," I said.

"I've never heard them say any of this," Brigitte said.

I peeked through one of the pinholes. Beef and Professor Camponi were in the lobby, talking. "They must have just overheard it. That's why Beef wants to win so badly, so that she can sing for them. I guess she thinks they'll love her and she'll make it big."

"That is not going to happen now," Brigitte said. "She is so far in last place, she won't catch up."

"Because of the book of tricks," Henri added.

"Because of me," I said. I hadn't played fair, and I'd ruined this woman's dream. Sure, I wanted to win, but I felt terrible about my little maneuver.

22

We waited until the lacrosse team once again passed through the lobby, creating total chaos. Étienne might have seen me scoot out with the last cage, but by then we were in the clear.

Henri and I waited outside the hotel for the pet-mobile, which Brigitte had parked around the corner. Her preferred parking didn't last overnight.

People pointed down the boulevard, so I figured it was approaching. I saw the snout first.

Did she really have a pig in that minivan?

A voice behind me asked, "Pig day?"

"Looks that way," I said to Knit Cap, who'd walked up next to me.

"Should I ask about the birds?" He nodded toward the cages on the sidewalk next to us.

"I wouldn't."

"Fair enough." He strummed and sang, "Fair is fair. Hair is hair. And I'd know you anywhere."

"Hey! Look at you go. Good job with the rhymes."

"You were right. It's a good way to start." He whipped the blue pages out of his back pocket. "Filled all these pages with rhyming lyrics."

"Then you're ready for lesson two."

"Lay it on me," he said.

"Here it is: Not everything has to rhyme."

"Hmmm, really? So, I could do something like . . ." He played a few chords.

> *"Run away,*
> *Be free,*
> *Be yourself,*
> *And leave your worries behind."*

In a way it didn't matter what he sang, because his voice was so hypnotic. But the chords were soothing and the lyrics flowed with them perfectly. "That's exactly what I meant," I said. "You could write all along, couldn't you?"

"I used to. I surely used to, but I've had a block that I couldn't get past for a long time. Your idea of rhymes and a scratch pad were just enough to unplug the logjam in my brain," he said. "Thanks a lot."

"You are very welcome. Maybe someday you'll write a song about me?"

"Maybe I will." He strummed a few notes.

I smiled because I liked them. They were fun and upbeat and kind of caught the essence of me.

Brigitte honked the petmobile horn at me. And, yup, it oinked!

"That's my cue," I said. "I gotta fly."

"To the last clue?"

"How do you know it's the last one?" I asked.

"Oh, I don't. It was just intuition." He picked at the strings and strolled down the street, singing about a girl. It sounded like the girl could be me.

Henri had loaded the birds in with . . . wait for it . . . a pig. The van was stuffed.

"Where to?" Brigitte asked.

I still felt bad about Beef, but we couldn't both win. It was going to be hard enough for just me to win. "To the next clue," I said. "I'll read it again. '*XX* marks the spot. Number eighty-three is the place. In the Garden of Names.'"

"Let me see *le papier*, please," Henri said. He looked at the paper. "This is not *XX*. It is how we number the *arrondissements* around Paris—they are like sections, or neighborhoods. It is Roman numbers. We need to go to the twentieth *arrondissement*."

"Awesome. Could eighty-three be a street? Like Eighty-Third Street?" I asked.

"Our streets are not numbered," Brigitte said. She cracked her window.

"*Mon Dieu*. What is the smell?" Henri asked. He rolled his window too. And then I did the same.

"*Excuse-toi*, Norman," Brigitte said to the pig. "Sorry, that happens after breakfast sometimes."

"Where is he going?" I asked.

"What do you mean?"

"I mean, where are you dropping him? Does he have a tap lesson or snorting practice or something?" I asked.

"No. He likes to ride around with me. It is his big day out. One day a week is Norman's Day of Fun," Brigitte said.

The birds said, "Day of fun!" "Day of fun!"

Great, I get to spend the whole day with Norman the

farting pig. Poor Henri was in the backseat, closer to him. Right now he hung his face out the window and made no indication he was coming back in anytime soon.

"If eighty-three isn't a street, what could it be?" I wondered aloud.

"Section eighty-three!" "Flowers to section eighty-three!" "Carnations!" "Section twenty-four!" "Section nineteen!" "Flowers!"

"What are they talking about?" I asked Brigitte.

"I do not know. Something from the flower cart, I think," Brigitte said.

"They seem to know section eighty-three."

"Section eighty-three!" "Section thirty-four!" "Tombstone!"

"Flowers on a tombstone?" I asked them.

"Carnations!" "Roses!" "Pansies!" "Tombstone!"

"Of course," Brigitte said. "The flower cart goes to Père-Lachaise, the biggest and oldest cemetery in Paris. The graveyard and gardens are divided into sections that are numbered."

"The Garden of Names," Henri said, "is like a garden of names on the tombstones."

"Makes sense to me," I said. "Let's go."

"Let's go!" "Let's go!" "Let's go!"

23

Brigitte extended a ramp from under the van for Norman to walk down.

"What are you doing?" I asked.

"It's Norman's Day of Fun. He won't have much fun locked in a petmobile all day, will he?"

Norman waddled down the ramp, and Brigitte strapped on a leash.

"The birds?" Henri asked.

"Bring one cage. They can sit on the flower cart, if it is here."

Henri said to the birds, "Who wants to come?"

"Come!" "Who!" "Who wants!"

He scrunched his mouth from one side to the other, clearly having trouble deciding which birds should come along. He pointed to them. "Eeny, meen—"

I grabbed the cage closest to the door and ran on ahead.

We found Monsieur Cliquot at the entrance to Père-Lachaise Cemetery. He kissed Brigitte on each cheek and took the cage from me. "*Bonjour*, Marlène. *Bonjour*, Jacqueline. *Bonjour*, Gary . . ." He greeted each of the birds by name as he let them out of their cage and perched them on top of the cart while they stretched their multicolored wings.

"*Bonjour*, Norman." He gave Norman the tops of some red carnations to eat.

"Will they let him inside?" Brigitte asked Monsieur Cliquot.

He gave her a small bouquet of yellow roses. "Get your ticket from the first teller. That is Monique. Give her these and she'll let him in."

"Thank you," Brigitte said. "I'll bring the other birds home later."

"*D'accord.*" He wished us luck with the rest of the hunt.

Brigitte gave Monique the flowers as Monsieur Cliquot

had advised, and voilà, pigs were welcome to roam the Père-Lachaise grounds.

With map in hand, we set out for section eighty-three, with Norman leading the way. Someone needed to explain in pig language that we were racing against the clock here. Norman checked out every smell the way you'd expect a dog to, and he nibbled flowers off the grave sites, generating dirty looks. At this rate it was going to take us forever to find section eighty-three. We had major ground to cover!

This cemetery was bigger, and more beautiful, than any I'd ever seen. I estimated that the walk to section fifty-two was probably a mile. Norman slowed down, and I expected that soon he'd need to rest. I plucked a few dead flowers from a grave and used them to lure Norman along. "Come on, boy. Good pig," I said, while I was thinking, *Just hurry up, you stupid pig!*

"Many famous people are buried here," said Henri.

"Like who?"

"Chopin and Molière," Henri said.

"I know Chopin was a great musician, but I don't know Molière," I said.

"That is because you are not French," Brigitte said. "Molière was a very famous playwright and actor. You probably know Jim Morrison."

"I've heard of him," I said.

"He was an American musician. Very popular," Brigitte explained. "Ah, section eighty-three," she announced.

It was not hard to find the grave we were meant to find because it was surrounded by royal blue shirts. Camera flashes snapped in our faces as we approached.

We were first! Even with the pig slowing us down, we'd won!

But then I saw Jean-Luc, Sabine, and Robert talking to Murielle duPluie. They smiled broadly when they saw us.

Seriously? My heart dropped.

Now we wouldn't get the tickets or backstage passes, and I wouldn't be featured on the French news.

A girl in blue said, "You are the first team to arrive with a pig."

"But the second team to arrive," I pointed out glumly.

"Yes, second. Second is good. Only the first and second get a chance at the box," she said.

Wait, what? "The box?" I asked.

"Yes. The game isn't over for you," she said. "There is one more challenge, and only the first two teams get to try it."

"Are you kidding?" Robert asked. "We were here first!"

"So you get to try with the box too." She smiled like this was exciting news, but Jean-Luc, Sabine, and Robert glared at her. Clearly, they hadn't seen this twist coming.

Murielle duPluie looked into the camera, shining her white teeth, and said, "It seems this contest is not over, Paris."

A microphone appeared in my face. "Hi there," she said to me. "Murielle duPluie with *Music News*. What are your names?"

I stared into the camera. "We are Gwen—from the US—and Henri and Brigitte—"

Brigitte interrupted me. "From Boutique Brigitte— Pour les Petits Animaux."

Murielle ignored her and asked me, "How does it feel?"

"It's amazing, like, with a capital *A*," I said. "I am so happy to be representing my country at this event. I mean, we're talking front row, and backstage passes!"

"Are you aware that Shock Value has sweetened the deal?"

"Sweetened?" Was that even possible?

She reached down and held up two identical boxes. Each had four drawers. The outside of each drawer had a different type of lock. "The first team to unlock all four of these gets an additional bonus ticket and invitations to a VIP reception with the band after the concert, in their greenroom. That's a total of five tickets!"

"With the band?" I repeated.

"Yes! Like a private party!" Murielle confirmed. Then she added, "Of course, I'll be there too." She pointed to the boxes. "You'll see that each of these drawers is locked. You need to use all the clues you've gathered so far to open them."

She gave one box to Robert, Jean-Luc, and Sabine, and the other to us. "The clock is going to start." The Shock Value rep gave Murielle duPluie a nod. "Now!"

I took our box and set it on the tombstone. "Okay." I pointed to a lock on one of the drawers. "This one looks like a regular keyhole," I said. I took the ribbon from my neck. "Easy, as long as this key works." I slid it in the hole and turned.

Click.

The door slid open, and inside was one Shock Value ticket.

"One down," I said.

Henri looked down.

"It's an expression," I said. "It means we're done with one."

Brigitte studied the other three. "What do you think about those?"

One of them was a hole about the size of a dime. Another was a number pad, one through ten. The last was a twisting combination lock.

I glanced a few feet away at Sabine, Jean-Luc, and Robert, who were also huddled around their own set of locks, whispering. "Where are the other clues?" I asked Brigitte.

Brigitte took them out of her pocket. "We have la place de la Concorde, the Statue of Liberty, and then the one that led us here."

"The Statue of Liberty and cemetery both have numbers, but not la place de la Concorde," I said. "Do you have the obelisk?"

She reached into her lab coat pocket, where, of course, she had the obelisk, and probably a shower cap, crowbar, and bottle of maple syrup.

"Do you want to do it?" I asked her, and pointed to the dime-size hole.

Brigitte slid the model monument into the dime-size hole and turned it.

Click.

"Two down," Henri said.

"Now the numbers. The twisting combination of my gym locker is three numbers."

"Then let's use the clue for the cemetery. It is the twentieth *arrondissement* and section eighty-three. We need a third number," Brigitte said.

"Is there a grave number?" All three of us looked

around. There wasn't. "Row?" Nothing. "How about year? When did he die?" I indicated the grave we were standing at.

Brigitte looked. "Last year."

I tried that combination of numbers, but it didn't work. I looked over to see how Robert, Jean-Luc, and Sabine were doing. They were already on the last drawer—the number pad. We were so close.

Think, Gwen, think.

"How about his age?"

"Whose?" Brigitte asked.

"The dead guy."

It took her a few seconds to calculate. "Twenty."

"Oh, that's so young. Poor guy." I tried twenty, eighty-three, twenty.

Click.

It opened.

The third ticket was in the drawer.

"Let's try the GPS coordinates on the number pad," Brigitte said.

"Yeah. Yeah." I waved my hand in front of the number pad. "Hurry!"

Jean-Luc, Robert, and Sabine were arguing. It looked like they had the Statue of Liberty clue, but maybe it was ripped up, or someone had thought it was trash.

Whatever had happened to it, now there was a section of paper missing, so they didn't have all the coordinates. The boys were yelling at her in fast French. She worked her phone. Probably to find the GPS numbers.

Brigitte referred to the paper and pushed in the keys. It opened easily. We had the fourth ticket!

"You did it!" the Shock Value rep said, and gave us the fifth and final ticket.

All three of us shot our hands in the air. "Done!" I yelled. And I launched into a hip-rotating happy dance complete with hands swinging over my head. Brigitte and Henri copied me, although we probably could have benefited from a little practice. We all high-fived.

"Belly bump?" Henri asked Brigitte.

She took a step back and walked into him for a chest bump, but once she hit Henri, she fell flat on her back.

Henri and I reached down and helped her up. She brushed dirt off her butt.

"We won!" I yelled to both of them again, because it was worth saying again and again. "We WON!"

"Bravo!" Murielle duPluie cried, and dragged her cameraman over to us. "Are we ready to roll?" she asked him.

"Ready. And . . . action."

24

"This is Murielle duPluie reporting live from Père-Lachaise Cemetery, where the American underdog Gwen Russell and her friends have just won the contest for tickets to Shock Value's special one-night engagement."

She put the mic into my face again. "How does it feel?" she asked—her signature question.

"*Fantastique!*" Brigitte said.

"*Formidable!*" Henri said.

"Oink," Norman snorted.

"Incredible!" I yelled. "I cannot wait to meet Winston, Alec, and Glen." Then I added, "U-S-A!"

"I'll be reporting all the backstage action from the VIP reception at the concert tomorrow." She paused and flashed her perfect smile.

The cameraman said, "Cut! That's great!"

"*What?*" Jean-Luc yelled at Murielle duPluie. He looked at the Shock Value lady and again asked, "*What? Are you kidding me?*"

"I can translate," I said. "I mean, if you wanted me to."

Jean-Luc got just an inch from my face. "No," he said. "I do not need a translation." Then Jean-Luc took a step backward, landing his foot right into a pig present that Norman had so perfectly placed at his feet.

Good pig!

"Aw! Gross!"

Robert said, "You are not getting into my car with those shoes."

"So disgusting!" Sabine said.

Jean-Luc said, "Get that stupid pig out of here."

"Or *you* could just leave," Brigitte suggested. "We still have to talk to the Shock Value people about winner business."

Jean-Luc harrumphed and walked away, sliding his feet on the grass.

Brigitte, Henri, and I enjoyed a high five, and we all petted Norman. After a short meeting with the Shock Value people to sort out all the deets for the next day, we began walking back to the petmobile.

"OMG!" I said. "This is just perfect. I made the news, I won the contest, and now I get to attend a VIP reception with the band."

If it was so perfect, why did I feel bad? One word: Beef.

"The only thing that could be better is if Clay Bright was there," Brigitte said.

"Too true," I said.

Henri said, "I wonder why he vanished and ran away."

"Maybe it was all too much, the pressure," I said. "And he just wanted to leave . . . to leave and . . ."

"What?" Henri asked. "Leave what?"

"His worries behind," I said. "And fly away." I get quiet, allowing my thoughts to race around the inside of my head.

Henri and Brigitte didn't notice my silence and kept talking. Brigitte said, "I guess we'll never know what happened to him."

I didn't respond right away. "We could ask him," I said.

"Ask who what?" Brigitte asked.

"We could ask Clay Bright why he disappeared," I said. "I know where to find him."

25

We went back to the Hôtel de Paris and walked up the boulevard to my friendly neighborhood guitarist.

"You're him," I said to Knit Cap.

"Who?"

"You're him!" I said again.

"Who?"

"Clay Bright," I said.

Henri studied him closely. "And you are not missing."

"It took you long enough to figure it out," he said. "I thought you were, like, a huge Shock Value fan."

"I am! But look at you. You're hanging out on the street. AND I thought you were missing!" I said. "What are you doing here?"

"This is my life now. It's all about music. That's what I was born to do."

"Being in the world's most popular band wasn't doing that for you?" I asked.

"It wasn't about the music anymore. It was photo shoots and perfume and T-shirts. Heck, I started buying music instead of writing my own. That was the last straw for me."

"So you just hang out here every day?"

"Yup. You know, I've been playing here for a year and Beef never recognized me."

"The costume is *très bien*," Henri said.

"Thank you. My mom made me the cap. You know, no one actually told me I was good or had real talent before you came along. It was always 'how many arenas can you sell out' or 'make sure you don't cut your hair before our next photo shoot.' It was never about the actual music. And you helped me get past my writing block." He strummed a few chords and began singing the most beautiful lyrics about making friends with strangers and being found.

"That's amazing," I said. "You're better than ever!"

"I don't know how I can thank you."

"I do," I said.

"Just ask," Clay said. "What can I do?"

"Get me another ticket to tonight's concert."

"Another?"

"Oh, yeah, we kinda won the contest!" I said.

"That's great! That's exactly what you wanted."

"It totally is."

"You are going to have an awesome night." He paused and crinkled his brow like he was thinking deeply. "Man, I miss those guys."

"You might have the chance to see them sooner than you think."

"Why?"

"I'd like you to help me get Beef in front of Shock Value," I said. "To give her the opportunity for a break."

"How will I do that?"

"By asking Alec, Winston, and Glen," I said.

"You mean, you want me to come out of hiding?" Clay asked.

"You're ready," I said. "Don't you think?"

Before he could answer, Brigitte asked, "Can you do a commercial for Boutique Brigitte—Pour les Petits Animaux? I mean, after you come out of hiding, of course."

"Sure," he told Brigitte. "But can it wait until next week?"

142

"That would be okay," she said.

"So, you'll do it?" I asked.

"It's time for me to fly back," he said. "Home to my boys. Let's go tell them."

"Tell the boys? As in Alec, Winston, and Glen?" I asked. I couldn't believe I was going to get to meet them, like, today.

Clay nodded. "We'll have to swing by my house first so I can change my clothes."

"Then *allons-y* to your house," Brigitte said. "I'll drive."

"Seriously?" Clay asked. "In the pet van?"

He was going to need a limo or something. He was Clay Bright. He was used to traveling in style.

"I've always wanted to ride in that thing," he said. "Is the snake in it?"

"No. But we can get her," Brigitte said. "She is such a pretty snake."

"Too true," Clay added. He secured his guitar in the case and clicked it shut.

On the way to the van Henri asked him, "Your mom has seen you since you have disappeared?"

"It would be pretty weird if she made me a sandwich every day but couldn't see me."

"Who else knows?"

"Just my mom. And, now, you guys."

He helped Brigitte with Norman's ramp, then got in.

"After my house, we'll go find the boys," Clay said. "They're the ones who can get you the ticket you need."

"You know where they are?" I asked. "You haven't talked to them in a year."

"I know all of their habits."

"So where are they?"

"Uncle Alphonse's garage. He lives in Essonne."

"You know who is on the way to Essonne?" Brigitte asked.

Clay nodded, then asked, "Is Fifi here?"

"No, but we can get her too. And we'll have to bring the birds!"

"Oh, yes. Please," Clay said. "Let's get them all."

Seconds later, Sylvie was in the van, hanging around Norman's neck like a scarf. Before I knew it, Fifi was sitting in Henri's lap, licking his face. She wasn't snug in her car seat because Clay Bright was in that space.

We left the animals in the car and went into a brick row home, where we found Clay's mother in the living room, sitting at a drum set. "Hi, honey," she said.

He gave her a kiss. "Hi, Ma. This is Henri, Gwen, and Brigitte. They just won the Shock Value contest. They need an extra ticket for some lady named Beef so she can play for the boys and maybe get her big break into musical stardom."

"Sounds good, honey." She pulled headphones over her ears. "I made tuna sandwiches." She jammed on the drums. Terribly and loudly.

Clay said, "Just give me a sec." He really was only gone for a sec, and when he returned, the only thing he'd changed was his cap. He took sandwiches out of the refrigerator and put them into a brown paper bag.

Clay lifted one of her earphones. "Wanna come?" he asked his mom.

"You're going to see the boys?"

He nodded.

"And not hide anymore?"

He nodded again.

"Sounds like a hoot." She put her drumsticks down and unplugged the earphones without taking them off. On the way out the front door she grabbed a white button-up sweater that looked like a librarian's. It didn't go with her cheetah-print leggings and spiky heels.

"Nice ride," she said when she saw the petmobile. She stuck her hand out, waiting for someone to put something in it. When no one did, she looked at us. "Keys?"

"It is my pet van," Brigitte said.

"Cool. I like it. But I'll drive. I always drive," she said.

Clay confirmed, "She always drives."

Brigitte took out the keys, but before she could give them to Mrs. Bright, the woman snatched them and got in the van. As we were still piling in, she peeled out. I fell into the seat with Henri, and Norman squealed.

Mrs. Bright yelled back, "Buckle up, amigos!" And floored it.

Finally, someone who could drive!

Mrs. Bright whizzed around corners, changed lanes, and honked the oinker generously. She appeared to know exactly where she was going. We left the city of Paris for the first time and traveled along the hilly French countryside. The grass was dark green, and slender fir trees lined both sides of the narrow road for miles. We all managed to crack our windows to let fresh air in and stale pig smell out. The animals were quiet and sniffed at the new scents in the air; even Sylvie gently swayed her head from side to side over Norman's shoulder. The pet van followed a sign with an arrow pointing toward Essonne.

Essonne was a picturesque village with many gardens, small rivers, and bridges. There were more bicycles than cars on the gravel streets, but that didn't slow down Mrs. Bright, who took tight turns and kicked dirt out from under the van's tires.

Brigitte held on to a hanging hook near the car

window with one hand and braced herself on the dash-board with the other for the entire ride. I was sure she wanted to say something, but except for a few whimpers, nothing left her mouth.

Mrs. Bright skidded into the unpaved driveway of a small stone cottage with white shutters and beautiful window boxes filled with colorful wildflowers. There was a trellis adorned with grapevines, underneath which sat a wrought-iron table and chairs. Sitting in the chairs were Winston, Glen, and Alec!

They saw Mrs. Bright and hopped up to greet her. Then they saw three strangers get out of a van, and last, they saw Clay. Their eyes widened in shock.

"No way!" Alec yelled, and ran into Clay's arms.

"*Incroyable!*" Winston ran his hands through his hair over and over.

"I should kick your butt right here, right now, man," Glen said. "But I'm just so glad to see you, I'll do it later."

"It's a date," Clay said, and he hugged his friend. "Look, guys, I know you probably have a lot of questions, and I'll tell you everything, but I need a favor."

"Now?" Alec asked.

"I guess it doesn't have to be *right* now, but since I'm here . . ."

"It's just that Murielle duPluie is on her way here to

do an interview. You know, a sit-down thing before the concert," Glen said. I loved that Glen talked like a New Yorker. If I wasn't at a beautiful cottage in a village outside of Paris with the most popular band in the world, I might have been a little homesick.

"An interview?" Clay asked. "That sounds perfect."

"For what?"

"A public reappearance?"

26

The petmobile was hidden.

Norman roamed and nibbled the grass with Sylvie on his neck. The two had become fast friends.

Winston's uncle Alphonse spoke to the birds who were still in the van in French and let them sit on top of the trellis to enjoy the sun.

Fifi had little interest in the country, and stayed glued to Henri's lap in the cottage kitchen, where we drank cappuccino. Uncle Alphonse didn't talk much, but rather busied himself around the kitchen, wiping, straightening, and refilling our cups. He pulled up a paint-chipped stool and motioned for Clay to sit on it. Then he took a razor from a drawer, wiped it on his pants, and went to work on Clay's beard.

When we heard Murielle duPluie's news van on the gravel, we spied out the window: She shook hands with the three current members of Shock Value and explained, "This is going to be live."

"That's right, man. Just like a good concert," Glen said.

Murielle duPluie looked at the cameraman. "Are we ready, Kevin?"

"Ready. And . . . action!"

"This is Murielle duPluie, and I'm coming to you live from Shock Value's secret practice location." She sat between the three handsome musicians under the trellis. "Are you guys excited about tomorrow's big show?" She put the mic in front of Glen, who seemed like the leader.

Glen said, "That's an understatement. This is going to be truly epic."

DuPluie asked, "More than usual? How come?"

Alec moved the mic in front of his own mouth. "I guess the best thing we could do is show you," he said. "You're gonna love this."

"Yes. We'll show you." Winston stood. "Come out, *mon ami*," he called to Clay.

Clay Bright walked out of Uncle Alphonse's cottage. His hair had been cut and his beard shaved, he wore a clean shirt tucked in, and a guitar hung on his back. He looked like a totally different person. The Clay Bright everyone knew and loved.

Murielle duPluie stared at Clay. Her lips didn't move. Shock? Amazement? Awe? It was anybody's guess, but the famous Murielle duPluie froze once she saw Clay Bright.

"He's returning for the concert," Glen said, helping her out.

Alec asked, "You're back, buddy. So great to see you. Where the heck have you been?"

"Sorry, but I needed to run away for a while, to find the music again. It's hard to explain, but I'd lost it," he said. "But I'm back now, and I missed you guys. And I missed the fans."

"So did you find it? Have you been writing?" Glen asked.

"I did," Clay said. "And yes, I have been writing quite a lot. Want to hear something new?"

"Would we?" Glen looked at Murielle duPluie. "What do you think? Would your viewers like to hear a new Shock Value song from Clay Bright, who has just returned to his band?"

"Uh-huh," she said, still in her frozen smile.

"Great!" Clay played a short section of the song about running away. "I'll be playing that one tonight," he said to Glen.

Murielle duPluie finally cleared her throat and looked into the camera. "There you have it. Musical history. Clay Bright is back and will rejoin Shock Value tonight," she said. "Follow me, Murielle duPluie, on *Music News* live throughout the evening. Remember, you heard it here first." She didn't move her stare from Clay.

Kevin, her cameraman, said, "And . . . cut."

27

The petmobile was loaded with me, Brigitte, Henri, and Natalie—Professor Camponi's granddaughter. We gave her one of the extra front-row tickets that we'd gotten for opening all the boxes. We gave Beef the fifth and final VIP ticket. For this event Brigitte had agreed, reluctantly, to leave any nonhuman friends behind. "Fifi will be so sad to miss it," Brigitte had said.

"We'll tell her all about it," I'd said. She didn't feel good about it until Henri suggested that we record parts of the concert and play it back for Fifi later.

I recognized the arena, the Palais Omnisports de Paris-Bercy (the locals called it POPB), from my tour books. It had a unique pyramidal shape and really cool walls that were actually covered with sloping lawns.

Brigitte navigated the van into the crowded parking lot and rolled down the window to pay the attendant for parking.

"*Bonjour*, Brigitte," said the parking attendant.

"*Bonjour*, Monsieur d'Argent. How is the little angel?"

"Ah, *très bien*. He is getting big." He handed her a bright red VIP parking sticker. "Put this on your window and you can park anywhere."

"*Merci*, but you see, I have two more buses behind me. One is from the Hôtel de Paris, and the other one carries a very noisy lacrosse team."

He stretched his neck around the petmobile and looked at the two buses behind us. "Ah! I see. Shock Value told me about them. They will have to sit with the maintenance crew in the mezzanine section. The view is obstructed, but it's the best we could do with the whole place sold out. We forgot that they would need to park." He scratched his bald head. "But for Brigitte, it is no problem." He took out two more red stickers. "I will give them these." He winked at her.

"*Merci*, Monsieur d'Argent. Thank you so much."

"For the girl who cleans Antonio's teeth, anything."

We drove on.

"Antonio?" I asked.

"Baby alligator," she said. "So cute and cuddly."

"Right," I agreed, "a cuddly alligator."

We flashed our backstage passes to every agent. Each one seemed like they were expecting us and the huge crowd of people who trailed along behind us. Of course, they couldn't all sit in the front row or go backstage. So Étienne and the apartment doormen who had driven in the hotel van were led to the balcony, while the lacrosse team and their families were directed to a long empty row up high in the nosebleed seats.

As we parted ways, I heard one of the lacrosse players say to Josh, "Your sister rocks."

Another player said, "She's cute, too."

Topher said, "Dude, gross."

I guess my new outfit, which Étienne had helped me select from the hotel store, looked good. It was a denim miniskirt and scoop-neck Shock Value T-shirt. A few days without contact sports and my legs were practically bruise-free. I'd taken some extra time to blow-dry my hair. It had never looked so good. It was amazing what some spray and a few rhinestone clips could do.

The last of our crowd of guests to walk away were Jean-Luc, Sabine, and Robert. That's right: I asked Shock Value for tickets for them, too. And they gave them to me because they were so appreciative that I'd convinced Clay to come back.

Sabine said, "I like your hair jewelry."

"Thank you," I said. "Enjoy the show."

Jean-Luc said, "You are okay, Henri, to get us these tickets."

"It does not mean that I will not beat you in the next game," he said.

"No, you won't," Jean-Luc said. "That will never happen again."

"Maybe we should bet—" Henri said.

I interrupted, "No. Let's not. Someone usually loses when you bet." I tugged Henri toward the front row. "Are you glad now that you invited them?"

"Maybe," he said. "They are going to get mad again when I score the next goal."

"Probably," I said, "Let's go."

Mr. Camponi's granddaughter, Natalie; Beef; Henri; Brigitte; and I were given the full backstage tour before being escorted to our seats—all of us except Beef, who was asked to stay behind with the band.

Natalie oohed and aahed at everything. From the

front row I saw Murielle duPluie in the wings, where she was reporting live.

Alec, Winston, and Glen took the stage. The audience cheered, "CLAY! CLAY!" After making us wait just long enough, Clay came onto the stage, and the four original members of the band, with Beef on the tambourine, launched into their most beloved song. The audience, including me, Henri, Brigitte, and Natalie, went nuts.

The set continued through Shock Value's classic songs. They danced, and the audience sang along. Everything about the concert was perfect.

Then Clay stood at the mic and said, "It's good to be back with my three bandmates and all of you here in Paris!"

The crowd screamed.

He continued, "Finding the courage to come back wasn't easy. I had a little help, actually. You see, I met a stranger who inspired me." The audience listened in silence. "This new friend also helped me find my way back to my love of writing music, and I think maybe I helped her discover something she didn't know about herself." Was he talking about me? "She had no idea that her voice rocked, because her older brothers . . ." He shaded his eyes from the spotlights and looked up into the mezzanine section. "They're up there somewhere.

Anyway, they told her she couldn't sing." He picked a guitar string. "Gwen, I want you to come up here and sing the song you wrote."

No! Freakin'! Way!

Was he seriously doing this?

"If it wasn't for you, I wouldn't be here right now." He started playing the familiar chords. "Let's rock."

Glen tapped the security guards in front of the stage. "Her," he told them, and pointed to me.

Two muscular security men lifted me onto the stage.

I tugged my skirt down and brushed a lock of hair over my ear.

The crowd cheered for me. For *me*! I thought I could hear JTC, but I couldn't see anyone because the lights totally blinded me.

Clay continued plucking at the sequence of chords. I swung my hips to the familiar and catchy tune.

Glen came over and hung a mic on a wire over my ear. He looked me in the eye and said, "Deep breath."

I took one.

Then he said, "You got this," and he strummed his guitar. Alec boomed on the drums, and Winston pounded on the keyboard.

I was so into the beat that when Clay started the first words, I joined right in. He lowered his voice and let me take over the song. "I could go to Japan!" I sang the whole verse; then Clay joined in to harmonize the second time through. The rest of the band hummed in the background. Beef clanked the tambourine.

I danced and walked across the stage, finally belting out, "If only I could fly!" Both of my hands were in the air.

Clay yelled, "Yeah!" and gave me a big hug. He whispered, "Thank you," in my ear. Then he announced, "Good night, Paris!"

The lights went out and I was escorted backstage. Natalie, Henri, and Brigitte were already in the greenroom. The band was right behind me.

Alec signed an autograph for Sylvie and one for Fifi, and Winston posed for countless pictures with Natalie. Even Beef was there. I listened to her live interview with Murielle duPluie.

Murielle duPluie asked, "So, how was it?"

"Well, you know, Murray—"

"Murielle," Murielle duPluie corrected her.

"It's like a nickname that I made for you," Beef explained.

"I don't like it, but how was it?"

"It was like I always imagined it would be. I can't thank Shock Value enough for giving me my big break. Now I have a question for you, Murray. Where do you get your hair done? Because it is fab and I was thinking of getting a little trim." She fluffed her very short waves.

Murielle duPluie's mic-less hand went to her hair. "Why, thank you. I can give you some names."

"Well, that would be appreciated," Beef said. She was definitely a smooth talker. "And how about that little lady?" She indicated me with her thumb. "My new friend. Wasn't she amazing?"

Murielle duPluie focused the mic on me, and Beef moved straight to a plate of shrimp cocktail.

"Hello, Gwen," she said. "I'm live with *Music News*. Can I ask you a few questions?"

"I'd like that," I said.

"I think the world is wondering, 'Who is Gwen Russell and what's her story?'"

"It's a super-simple story, really," I told Murielle duPluie. "I came to Paris and I made a wish on a lantern that I tossed off the cliff at la côte d'Albâtre."

"What was your wish?"

Henri interrupted, "Do not tell her. It will not come true."

"It's okay," I told Henri.

"Well?" Murielle duPluie asked.

"I wished for the best week ever in Paris."

"And did you have it?" she asked me.

"I got to spend time with my old friend and surrogate sister, Brigitte, and her gang of pets. I won the Shock Value scavenger hunt. I not only met the band, but I returned their friend and bandmate to them—not many people can say they've done something like that. He convinced me to start singing, and it turns out I'm pretty good. And"—I took Henri's hand—"I made a great new friend."

"So your wish came true?"

"You bet it did," I said. "Wait. Actually, don't bet. Someone usually loses."

The cameraman pushed in closer to Murielle duPluie. She stared straight into the camera, at her viewers, and said, "There you have it, music fans. A wish on a lantern ends in musical history. I'd say that's a successful trip to Paris."

28

The next day was my last in Paris. I couldn't believe it.

I entered the cozy lobby and watched tour group D gather by the podium to be briefed by Beef. The tour group was considerably larger than mine had been. It seemed that Beef's recent musical success attracted tourists. I noticed that in addition to her fanny pack and clipboard, she now also had her tambourine hanging from her belt.

Henri was leaning against a wall near the grand front door of the Hôtel de Paris. His hair was combed back and tied into a ponytail; his striped oxford was pressed and untucked. He had one hand shoved deep into a front pocket, and the other waved to me.

"Hi," I said. "You aren't working today?"

"No. Not today. Étienne gave me the day with no work."

"Off."

"Off what?"

"Off work. That's what we call a day with no work, a day off."

"Then off," he said. *"Allons-y."* Let's go.

"Where?"

"You aren't done with your great week in Paris."

"I'm not?"

"No. There's something you need to see." He took my hand. "Come on."

I went with him outside to the front of the hotel. I looked for Clay Bright, but he wasn't there. Then I looked around for the petmobile, but I didn't see it barking, squawking, or oinking nearby.

"Where is Brigitte?"

"She was picking up new rats for Sylvie."

"Yuck," I said.

"Yeah. Yuck."

Henri stopped walking at a yellow Vespa scooter and handed me a helmet from the back.

I said, "I don't think my mom—"

He put it on my head. "I already talked to her and JTC. The boys convinced her that you can go with me for an hour."

"Really?"

He buckled the strap and tapped the top of the helmet. "Really." He kicked a leg over the scooter and fastened his own helmet. "Get on."

I straddled the seat and wrapped my hands around Henri's waist. He flicked a switch and something with his foot, and we cruised down the boulevard. We stopped near the edge of the Seine—right near the fleet of tour boats I had seen when I had first arrived.

"A river cruise?" I asked.

"Oui," Henri said. He slid a plastic card out of his pocket. "A gift," he said. "From Professor Camponi. For taking Natalie to the concert." He waved me ahead of him onto the boat.

I stepped on and climbed up to the top deck, Henri following close behind.

The boat sailed down the river that flowed through the center of Paris. We went under what seemed like a million bridges. It was so cool to see the city we had been running around from the water—the Louvre, Notre Dame, and a bunch of other sights we hadn't gotten to see. Henri pointed to buildings and told me what he could about each.

"Guess what?" he asked me.

"What?"

"Les Bleus won the World Cup."

"So I guess that proves it," I said. "Lantern wishes come true whether you tell them or not."

He squeezed my hand and held it for the rest of the ride while we slowly sailed down the Seine.

Here's a sneak peek at another international adventure by Cindy Callaghan:

Pizza, pasta, and a little *amore!*

1

I'd been planning to be a counselor-in-training at Camp Hiawatha, but there was an issue with fleas, mice, lice, and snakes and the camp closing, leaving my summer *wide open*.

The only question was, what would I do with all my free time? Thankfully, my parents were able to make alternate plans.

"It's all set," my mom said.

"For real?" I asked.

"Totally for real," Dad confirmed. "Your great-aunt Maria can't wait to have you."

My great-aunt Maria was my dad's aunt, and she was more than *great*, she was my favorite relative in the adult category. She was sweet, nice, an amazing Italian cook, and she owned this insanely cute pizzeria. Plus, I always felt like she and I had some kind of special connection—like a bond or something. I can't really explain it exactly.

Oh, and that pizzeria she owned? It just happened to be in Rome. Rome, Italy!

Basically, Aunt Maria is all that and a plate of rigatoni, if you know what I mean.

"When do we leave?" I asked.

"Tomorrow morning," Mom said. "But this isn't going to be two weeks of sightseeing and touristy stuff. I told her you wanted to work."

"At the pizzeria?"

"Yeah," Dad said. "She's planning to teach you how to make her signature sauce."

"The secret sauce?" I asked in awe.

"That's the one," he added. "*I* don't even know how to make it."

"That's a major deal," Mom said.

Just then a girl who looked a lot like me—long dark curly hair, light skin, brown eyes, except she was taller, prettier, older, and more stylish—walked into our parents' room, where we were talking. A cell phone was glued to her ear.

"It's on!" I said.

"For real?" she asked.

"For real!"

She pumped her fist in the air. "I'll call you later. I'm going to Rome! *Ciao!*" She hung up the phone, looked at herself in the full-length mirror, fluffed her brown curly locks, and practiced, *"Buongiorno!"*

Maybe I should tell you who "she" is: My older sister, Gianna. She's like my best friend. There's no one I'd rather be with for two weeks in Rome. Next year she'll be a junior in high school, where she is most often seen with a glitter pen and scrapbooking scissors.

Me . . . not so much. I'm more of a big-idea gal. Then she builds or glues or sews or staples my ideas into reality.

This fall she'll start looking at colleges. She's excited about it, but the idea of her leaving home makes my stomach feel like a lump of overcooked capellini. Maybe some sisters fight, but Gi and I are tight. (Okay, *sometimes* we fight like sisters.)

Mom said to Gianna, "I told Lucy that you girls are going to work at the pizzeria."

"I love that place," Gianna said. "I hope it's exactly the same as I remember it."

"Do you think she still has Meataball?" I asked. I had visited Aunt Maria and her pizzeria years ago, and I vaguely remembered her cat.

"The cat?" Dad asked. "He has to be dead by now, honey. But maybe she has another cat."

"Gi, she's gonna teach me how to make her sauce."

"Just you?"

I shrugged. "Maybe she loves me more."

Mom said, "No. She loves you both exactly the same."

"Maybe," I started, "she wants me to take over the pizzeria when she retires, and I'll be the Sauce Master, the only one in the entire Rossi lineage who knows the ancient family signature sauce. Then, when I'm old, I'll choose one of my great-nieces to carry on the family tradition. And—"

Mom interrupted. "Lucy?"

"What?"

"This isn't one of your stories. Let's bring it back to reality."

"Right," I said. "Reality." But sometimes reality was so boring. Fiction—*my* fiction—was way better. I'm pretty sure I'm the best writer in my school, where I'm a soon-to-be eighth grader.

Gianna asked, "You're totally gonna teach it to me, right?"

"It depends on if I have to take some kind of oath that could only be broken in the event of a zombie apocalypse," I said.

Dad suggested, "And let's try to cool it with apocalypse-related exaggerations, huh? Aunt Maria probably doesn't 'get' zombies and their ilk."

"Roger that, Dad," I said.

"I'm going to pack," Gianna said. "I can bring a glue gun, right? That's okay on the plane, isn't it?"

"I'm pretty sure they have glue guns in Italy. Or maybe you could refrain from hot-gluing things for two weeks," Mom suggested.

"Ha! You're funny, Mom," Gianna said. "Don't lose that sense of humor while the two of us are spending fourteen days in Italy!"

Gi and I looked at each other. "ITALY!" we both yelled at the same time.

We would've screamed way louder if we'd had any idea how much this trip would change the future—mine, Gianna's, Aunt Maria's, Amore Pizzeria's, and Rome's.

2

※

STAMP!

The customs officer, who sat in a glass-enclosed booth, pounded his stamp onto Gianna's passport.

I slid mine through a little hole in the glass, and he did the same.

New stamps in our passports!

"Yay!" Me and Gi high-fived.

A few moments later my eyes caught a paper sign that said LUCIA AND GIANNA ROSSI.

The lady holding it wasn't Aunt Maria. She was as

different as possible from our older Italian aunt. She was young, maybe twenty-three, and was all bright colors and peculiarities. Her head was wrapped in a dark purple scarf with a long tail hanging down her back. Her sunglasses were splotched with mismatched paint, and her pants were unlike any that I'd ever seen: one leg was striped and short and snug (maybe spandex), while the other leg was flowery, long, and flowing (possibly silk).

We made our way over to her and her sign.

"Are you Lucia and Gianna?" she asked without a trace of an Italian accent. She was as American as me.

We nodded.

"Buongiorno!" She hugged us just like Aunt Maria would have: tight, and extra long. "I am Jane Attilio and I've come to take you to Amore Pizzeria. *Andiamo!"*

Gi and I looked at each other, unfamiliar with the word. Maybe she didn't know that we didn't speak Italian.

"Let's go!" Jane added with a big smile. With one hand she dragged my wheely suitcase. With the other she took Gianna's hand and led us out of the airport. "We're going to have an incredibly awesome two weeks."

Jane Attilio effortlessly crammed our bags into her small European automobile (a Fiat) and whizzed us— and I do mean "whizzed"!—through the streets of Rome.

While Jane's driving was fast, it was no crazier than everyone else's. I would've buckled up twice, if that was possible.

We passed ancient and crumbling buildings and statues, monuments and ruins. When traffic stopped, we were next to a big stone wall, where a very long line of people stood.

"What are they doing?" I asked.

"Behind that wall is Vatican City. Those people are in the queue to go in." Jane pointed to a half-moon of gigantic stone columns. "That plaza is Saint Peter's Square. See that big dome behind it? That's the Basilica. People travel very far to get in there."

"So cool," I said, and snapped a picture on my cell phone.

Jane navigated the roads onto a white marble bridge called the Ponte Principe Amedeo Savoia Aosta, which took us over the Tiber—a river that ran right through the middle of the city.

Finally Jane's little car halted at the end of a cobblestone alley. "Amore Pizzeria is down there," she said.

Gianna started getting her bags out of the car and setting them down on the street.

Jane said, "That's okay. Leave your bags. I'll drop them off at Aunt Maria's apartment. It's not far." She hugged us both again, real hard. "She is so excited to see you girls. You're all she's talked about since she found out you were coming." Jane got back into the car and yelled, "I hope you'll be able to cheer her up."

Why does she need cheering up?

3

Ahhh! I recognized the smells of roasting garlic and simmering tomatoes from my great-aunt Maria's signature secret sauce. I hadn't smelled it in years.

"Lucia! Gianna!" Aunt Maria called from the kitchen through a big rectangular opening in the wall. The hole was for passing hot food from the kitchen to the dining room. It had a ledge where the cook could set plates while they waited to be picked up. "The girls are here!" She shuffled out.

Aunt Maria looked older than I remembered; her

hair, which used to be black, was now peppered with gray. She grabbed hold of me—thankfully, her snug embrace hadn't changed. She switched to hug Gianna and then back to me again. Either she'd shrunk or I'd grown—maybe both—but now I was taller than her.

I said, "It's good to see you, too." After three rounds of embraces, Gianna and I were both dusted with flour from her hands and apron.

She stepped back and studied us from head to toe. "Look at you." She grew teary. "You are so *bellissima*, beautiful." She lifted the tomato-sauce-speckled apron and wiped her eyes. "I am so happy you girls are here. You are like a breath of the fresh air." She took us each by the hand and led us to a table. "Look at how skinny you are. I am getting you the pizza." She frowned at our figures, then hustled behind the counter. "Sit. Sit. It will take me one minute."

I hadn't been to Amore since first grade. Evan though I didn't remember the visit well, I knew the familiar scent of spices seeping out of the walls like ghosts of old friends.

Now the pizzeria looked worn, like Aunt Maria had tried to redecorate at some point but hadn't finished. Paint covered the exposed brick wall. The chairs and tables needed attention—they were chipped, stained, and a little wobbly.

A picture of my great-uncle Ferdinando hung in the center of a wall covered with framed photos that looked like they hadn't been dusted in months, maybe years. There was a ledge holding trinkets that seemed to be layered with a thin coating of Parmesan cheese.

Aunt Maria returned with two plates and three bottles of Aranciata (an Italian orange soda that I love!). Not sure why she had brought the extra bottle. *"Mangia, mangia,"* she said. "Eat, girls."

Crispy crust.

Aunt Maria's signature sauce.

Steamy, melty mozzarella cheese.

Ooey, gooey, cheesy, and crispy.

It was, like, delicious with an ice-cold glass of *mmmmm.*

We had totally hit the jackpot with these temporary summer jobs.

Let me tell you about Amore's pizza, because it's different from American pizza: first, they're round, not triangle, slices. It's like everyone gets their own small individual pie made specifically for them. And the toppings are different. The ones she brought out were smothered with roasted garlic.

"It's quiet in here," Gianna commented.

"*Sì*. There are not so much customers." Aunt Maria

sighed sadly. Maybe this is why she needed cheering up. "You like the pizza?"

"It's as good as I remembered," I said through a mouthful of cheese.

Aunt Maria nestled herself into a chair across from us and exhaled as she took her weight off her feet. "I have something to tell you." She looked us both in the eye. "You cannot work here."

Splat! Those words landed like a meatball plopped onto a plate of spaghetti.

"What?" Gianna and I asked together.

"Well, one of you can," she clarified. "But not both."

One of us has to go home? But we just got here!

"How come?" Gianna asked. "What's wrong? We promise we'll work hard."

"It's not that. It is the Pizzeria de Roma." Aunt Maria spat the name. "It's an old pizzeria in the piazza by the Fontana del Cuore." That's the Fountain of the Heart. "Now it has a big new flashy sign and shiny new forks," she said. "Everybody go there. They see it right there in the piazza!"

"How's their pizza?" I asked.

"You think I know?" She pinched her fingers together and flipped her wrist back and forth as she spoke. "I never go."

"Then how do you know that they have shiny forks?" I asked.

"Signorina Jane Attilio. She live upstairs." Aunt Maria pointed up. "She see them when she walk past."

Gianna and I looked at each other. "Are you going to send one of us home?" I asked.

"No. No. No. You stay. Signorina Attilio, she says one of you can help her. She is very busy."

"Oh, great," I said. "Let me guess. She works at a funeral home, or a toothpick factory, or vacuuming dirt out of USB ports?"

(I didn't think there was really any such thing as a toothpick factory.)

"What is this 'ports'? No. No," Aunt Maria said. "She is a tailor."

Gianna's eyebrows shot up. "Like, she makes things? I'm great at that."

"Sì?" Aunt Maria asked.

"Yes. See these jeans?" Gianna stood and showed the rhinestone embellishments on the back pocket. "I added them myself."

"*Bella!* You are good at the designs," Aunt Maria said, admiring the bling. "You will like to work with Signorina, sì?"

"I think I will."

"Then you are the one," Aunt Maria said to Gianna.

Phew! I would've skinny-dipped in the Fontana del Cuore before I'd have given up working at Amore.

At that moment, a boy walked in Amore's front door. Not just any kind of a boy. He was extremely cute, with a thick head of dark hair to match his thick arm muscles. He looked like he was Gianna's age. Gianna's eyes popped out of her skull at the sight.

"*Buongiorno,*" he waved. "I am Lorenzo."

"You!" Aunt Maria pointed at him. "I know who you are. You do not come in here!"